APR 0 5 2017

Belief

MAYANK BHATT

MAWEN乙I
HOUSE

We acknowledge the support of the Canada Council for the Arts for our publishing program. We also acknowledge support from the Government of Ontario through the Ontario Arts Council.

Cover art: *Decoy, self-portrait, 1966* by Charles Pachter
Cover design by Sabrina Pignataro

Library and Archives Canada Cataloguing in Publication

Bhatt, Mayank, author
	Belief / Mayank Bhatt.

ISBN 978-1-927494-80-6 (paperback)

	I. Title.

PS8603.H388B45 2016   C813'.6   C2016-904502-1

Several places described in the book are real. However, this is a work of fiction and resemblances to any persons are unintended.

Printed and bound in Canada by Coach House Printing

Mawenzi House Publishers Ltd.
39 Woburn Avenue (B)
Toronto, Ontario M5M 1K5
Canada

www.mawenzihouse.com

I was born a Hindu, no doubt. No one can undo the fact. But I am also a Muslim because I am a good Hindu. In the same way I am also a Parsi and a Christian too.

—MAHATMA GANDHI, 30 May 1947

for

Mahrukh and Che

I

The Terror Files

One

"Ammi, I did nothing wrong," Rafiq said, turning to his mother, Ruksana, his voice breaking. She gave him a pained, helpless look, tears streaming down her full cheeks. From his other side, his father, Abdul, gently spoke up, "Beta, there is still time, tell the police everything you know."

Rafiq quickly turned to glare at him. "Abba, I am not involved."

Handcuffed, his face full of emotion, Rafiq stood at the door of their house, pleading with his parents, pleading with the world—yet defiant. He was a young man in his early twenties; he was of medium height, with a trimmed beard, and was wearing a blazing red hoodie, a pair of blue jeans, and white sneakers with red laces. Two white officers of the Peel Regional Police then frogmarched him briskly down the driveway. Arriving at the awaiting police car, they nodded at their colleague Ravindar Singh, who opened the rear door, pushed Rafiq inside, and followed him in. The car eased down the suburban road and sped away.

It was early dusk in late fall and the porch lights were on. The recently built townhouse, which the family had named Manzil, meaning "Destination," stood on Brandon Gate Drive in the Malton district of Mississauga. Traffic on the secluded street was sparse—the odd car returning home from work, the curious driver staring at the motley group outside the lit-up house.

As the cruiser disappeared down the road, Ruksana broke down and buried her head into her daughter Ziram's shoulder. Abdul Latif, barely able to hold his composure, stood beside his son-in-law Jameel. With the Latifs were their friends and neighbours—Kartar and his wife Harminder, a Sikh couple. Kartar led the family inside. The living room was brightly lit with three floor lamps, and three more lamps on the ceiling fan.

"Beta, you sit. You need to take care," Ruksana told her daughter, who was two months pregnant. She herself went and piously touched the large golden frame of the photograph of Kaaba on the wall above the TV, and then put her fingers to her forehead. A large couch, a settee, and a chair upholstered in a batik print occupied most of the room. A faux Kashmiri carpet, which Ruksana had found at a garage sale, partly covered the floor. A glass-topped table held a crystal vase filled with plastic pebbles and flowers.

Abdul took off his beige corduroy jacket and flung it upon the backrest of the chair, then rolled up the sleeves of his plain white shirt and sat down heavily, with a sigh. He was fifty-two years old, with a prominent jaw and elongated nose. A small man, he was clean-shaven; his small eyes looked diminished behind the black-framed glasses, and his knitted brows added years to his face. His hairline had receded, the hair now more grey than black.

Ruksana, wearing a beige woollen sweater over her pale blue salwaar-kameez, had sat down at the dining table. Unlike her husband, she had aged gracefully. She had a thin curved nose and large eyes that formed perfect circles on her round face. Both her children had these features, though she often wished they had Abdul's fair skin.

Ziram stood beside her mother, gently rubbing her back.

"We shouldn't have called the police," Ruksana spoke up in a husky voice. "Now they will frame him even if he is innocent."

"Maybe they will let him go after routine questions," Abdul mumbled without conviction.

—⁊⁊—

Earlier that evening, Abdul and Ziram had discovered a folder slugged "Brampton" on Rafiq's computer in the upstairs study. Originally Ziram's bedroom, it had been turned into a study after she married Jameel and moved out. It was the startling contents of the folder that had led to the evening's developments.

Both Ziram and Jameel worked at a community centre in Malton.

For the last couple of months, since she became pregnant, Ziram and her husband would stop over at her parents' home in the evening after work. She taught her father to use the computer, while Jameel sat in the living room watching TV or chatting with his mother-in-law. Abdul had recently been laid off by the auto parts firm in Etobicoke where he had worked ever since he came to Canada. That evening Ziram was explaining to her dad a short cut for transferring files when she saw the "Brampton" folder. She had seen it earlier, too, but hadn't paid any attention to it. Today, her curiosity got the better of her, and she clicked on it, though not without some hesitation.

A folder named "Emails" appeared, with two Word files below it. The first of the Word files was labelled 1-GA-15-Feb-2007. She opened it.

His glasses on the tip of his nose, Abdul peered at the monitor to take a closer look at the contents of the file. "What is it?" he asked.

"It's a message . . . " Ziram murmured uncertainly. "But why has he saved it?" It was an email from someone called Ghani Ahmed. As Ziram read it, she became still and took a deep breath.

She glanced up at her dad, and then turned back to the monitor.

"Oh my God, what the fuck is this?" she exclaimed, forgetting that she was sitting beside her father. "Look at this, Abba."

Abdul looked uncertainly at her; he took off his glasses and peered at the screen. He read:

```
This is the plan for Square One,
Mississauga. The bag will be placed
in the food court for maximum impact.
```

"What does it mean?" he asked, turning to his daughter, whose eyes were fixed on the monitor. He began to get a bad feeling.

"He received this message on February 15, 2007, that is, last year, from Ghani Ahmed," Ziram whispered.

"It doesn't matter when he got it and who sent it! What does it mean?" He got up from his chair. "Read the next one," he commanded.

Her heart racing, Ziram clicked on the file labelled 2-GA-29-Feb-2007. The contents spilled out on the screen.

"This one is about the Viva-YRT bus terminal at Finch," Ziram began.

"Read it to the end."

> As Salam Aleikum! This is 3rd in a
> series of 7 msgs. The device will
> be in a duffel bag and the carrier
> will reach Finch by the subway from
> Eglinton. He will walk to the VIVA
> YRT bus terminal. He will wear a black
> woollen jacket, which he will remove
> when inside the terminal. Underneath,
> he will have on a light blue, full-
> sleeves shirt, a Blue Jays jacket,
> blue jeans, and sneakers. He will chew
> gum while at the terminal. He will
> leave the duffel bag beneath a chair
> in the waiting lounge. This will have
> maximum impact. He will wait in the
> lounge for about 10 minutes, and then
> walk to the coffee shop at the termi-
> nal. He will buy coffee and walk out
> of the station, heading north to the
> parking lot of the strip mall at Yonge
> and Finch, and get into a turquoise
> green Toyota Corolla parked outside
> Canada Computers. More instructions
> will follow.

The message ended with,

> Avenge Canada's massacre of Muslims in
> Afghanistan! Avenge the massacre of
> innocent Muslims in Palestine, Iraq
> and Kashmir!

Ziram clutched at the edge of the desk. Her face was pale, her hand shaking. In a trembling voice, she said, "These messages are about bombing different places in Toronto, and some Ghani Ahmed guy has sent them. But why has Rafiq saved them?"

Abdul was too stunned to respond. His weak heart thudded inside him. He put his hand on Ziram's shoulder to steady himself. Having taken some moments to calm himself, he asked Ziram to print the two messages.

"Abba, who's this Ghani Ahmed?"

Even as he tried to comprehend what he had just seen, Abdul felt a shot of irritation at Ziram's proclivity to curse and her peculiarly broad and elongated way of pronouncing Indian names. He wanted to tell her, "It is Ghani not Ghhaanee." But that was not important right now. Who *was* this Ghani Ahmed?

He had no idea about his son's friends. He had rarely seen his son since he started working as a web designer at Wanderlust, a Brampton travel agency, three years ago. When Rafiq wasn't at his office, he was at his laptop in his basement bedroom or in the study upstairs, with a plate of kebabs, and a can of Coke. Ruksana had enforced a strict halal-food rule in Canada, and their modest means had ensured that Rafiq grew up eating only homemade food.

"Call your mother, she may know," Abdul said.

Ziram walked over to the landing at the stairs and shouted down to her mother to come up. Her voice came out as a shriek, causing even Jameel to scamper upstairs.

"Ammi, do you know if Rafiq has a friend called Ghani Ahmed?" Ziram asked, trying to control her frayed nerves and sound as calm as possible.

"No," Ruksana said, her eyes flitting between Ziram's and Abdul's worried faces. "What's going on?"

"Ammi, sit down." Ziram said, pulling out the chair from the computer table for her mother, and told her what she and her dad had discovered. Jameel read a few excerpts from the printouts. "He's bcc'd on these emails," he said, and passed them to Ruksana, who read them slowly, one by one.

"Call him home right now, let us talk to him," Ruksana said when she finished reading the messages.

Abdul called up Rafiq, who answered at the first ring. "Son, when are you coming home? We are waiting for you." Rafiq calmly told his father to have dinner and go to sleep. "I'll be late." He rang off, and Abdul looked around sheepishly. Ziram grabbed the phone from him and called Rafiq back. Before he could say anything, she snapped, "We've seen your emails, you better come home right now!"

"What emails?"

"Ghani Ahmed's."

There was a moment of silence at the other end, and then Rafiq spoke in a measured tone. "Give the phone to Abba." In the same tone, Rafiq told Abdul, "Abba, I'm coming home." Before Abdul could say anything, Rafiq hung up.

"Allah! What will happen now?" Ruksana said.

"I will call Kartar," Abdul said. Jameel guided everyone to the living room downstairs.

Kartar and Harminder, who lived two houses away, arrived at once. Kartar was a big man with hazel eyes and a scraggly salt-and-pepper beard. He wore a Sikh turban, which just failed to cover the lobes of his long ears. His wife Harminder was also tall, a fair-skinned, strong-boned woman with sharply chiselled features. She was wearing a plain pastel-shade salwaar-kameez, and her head was loosely covered with a dupatta.

"Are you sure?" Kartar asked, as he sat on the couch next to Harminder.

"We spoke to him," Ziram said softly. Abdul nodded.

They discussed whether Kartar should ask Ravindar, his nephew in the police, to come over. Ruksana wasn't sure, but after some pondering Abdul agreed.

Ravindar soon arrived. He didn't wear the Sikh turban or keep the characteristic beard or long hair. Premature balding had led him to shave his head. He was a tall, fair-skinned man with the buffed body of someone who worked out regularly; he had brown eyes, bushy eyebrows, and a prominent straight nose, and appeared quite intimidating.

Ravindar pored over the printouts for some minutes while the others waited, then stiffly asked Abdul if the family knew Ghani Ahmed. They all shook their heads.

"I'll have to inform my superiors. These messages could be part of a terrorist plot."

"What will the police do?" Abdul asked.

Ravinder paused, before replying, "Confiscate all the papers and the hard drive, and search your house."

There was an anguished silence in the room. Then Ruksana asked, "Will he be arrested?" her voice barely audible.

"We'll have to take him in. You should consult a lawyer. The police can provide you with legal-aid counsel."

"Let's talk to him before jumping to conclusions," Ruksana said.

—⁂—

They all had different expectations of Rafiq. Abdul, Ruksana, and Ziram hoped that he would have a simple explanation for the emails—they were just a game and meant nothing, there was no such person as Ghani Ahmed. Jameel hoped the situation wouldn't blow up into something big, or it could mar the promotion he was seeking at work. Ravindar anticipated a promotion at the end of it all; perhaps he'd become an inspector; and Ravindar's aunt and uncle Kartar and Harminder simply wished to go home.

Soon they heard a car arrive outside and the front door open. Rafiq gave a start at seeing them all gathered in the living room, grim looks on their faces. He darted nervous glances around the room, scratched his beard as he took off his shoes by the stairs. Ruksana fetched a glass of water for him, which he brusquely refused. He looked at Ravindar and then at his parents. He sat down on a chair at the dining table, facing them all.

"We asked Ravindar to come over to help us," Ziram said.

"You call the cops before you talk to me?" Rafiq said, his voice rising, his face a mix of anger, contempt, and disillusionment. He took off his hoodie, and kept it on his lap.

Ruksana, sitting next to him, tried to hold his hand but he shrugged her off.

"What did you expect us to do?" she asked calmly.

"Ammi, you won't get it," he said, dismissively.

"If you think we have misunderstood, we will ask Ravindar to leave," Abdul said. "But you have to tell us what all this means." By now he was convinced his son had been up to something gravely wrong. Those messages he had read weren't innocent. They were about killing people. He didn't want to say that out aloud in the presence of a policeman, but he wasn't going to let his son get away by throwing a tantrum. Rafiq fixed a steely gaze at him for a moment, and then sullenly looked down.

Ruksana pleaded, "Rafiq, we lost everything that was ours in India. But Saabji never speaks about it." Saabji was what she called her husband.

"He's used to being treated as a second-class citizen," Rafiq shouted, and threw his hoodie on the floor.

"So what should I have done? Set off bombs, and killed people?" Abdul retorted angrily.

Rafiq looked at his feet and twirled his toes.

Ravindar had hoped that Rafiq would talk to his parents, but that wasn't happening. "If you talk before the police team arrives, I promise you that whatever you say stays with me," he said.

Rafiq didn't respond.

"Do you know Ghani Ahmed personally? Is December 31 the D-Day? What are the targets?"

Again, Rafiq stared at his feet, and twirled his toes.

From the living room window, they saw a police cruiser drive up. There was a sound of footsteps and Ziram opened the door. Rafiq glanced at the two officers who stepped in, and then at his mother.

—w—

After the police team had sealed the study, and taken photographs, an officer told Rafiq, "I'm arresting you for working with a terrorist group." Then, according to legal provisions, he asked Rafiq and the family to call a lawyer, and if they didn't know or could not afford one, he told them they had a right to a legal-aid counsel.

At this point Rafiq looked scared and, looking around at his family, said, "What should I do? I've done nothing wrong."

"So why the hell did you keep quiet all this while? You should've said so earlier," Jameel replied, unable to hide his exasperation.

"Why did you call the cops before talking to me?" Rafiq said, his voice breaking. He was crying.

"Let me see if I can call Anita Persaud," Jameel said. He called the lawyer, whom he knew, on his cellphone, but there was no answer, and he left a message for her.

"We're taking him to Division 22. He'll be taken to the courthouse tomorrow morning for his remand," one of the officers said. "You can get a lawyer to go there, otherwise a duty counsel at the court will help you."

"We'll do something . . . don't worry," Ziram said anxiously, looking at Rafiq, feeling a sudden wave of compassion for her brother.

Two

The police team drove Rafiq to Division 22 police station in Brampton, where Ravindar and the officers led him along a corridor leading away from the main concourse. They reached a long, white, brightly lit oval room with four cubicles at the sides, into one of which they guided him. It had a square table, and a couple of bucket chairs facing each other. Ravindar motioned to the other members of the team to wait outside the cubicle.

Ravindar had no patience for the likes of Rafiq, but his job required him to demonstrate understanding. He often played the desi—the "fellow-Indian"—card with Indians or South Asians to build trust and help them open up during interrogation. He switched to Hindustani. "You know, it'll help everyone if you cooperate." Rafiq was surprised. He understood the language of his parents—they called it Urdu—but preferred not to speak it. He was aware that even for Ravindar speaking in Hindustani was not natural. He had an unnatural accent.

"Tell me what you know about this plot," Ravindar said, his elbows on the table, leaning forward.

Rafiq sat stiff and motionless, his fingers drumming the sides of his chair, staring at Ravindar's large shaved head.

"I'll talk to my lawyer," he mumbled.

Unable to conceal his annoyance, Ravindar got up and walked away. Another officer came in and took Rafiq's fingerprints, then led him out of the cubicle to the blank wall at the far end of the room to take his photograph.

"You'll be taken to the courthouse tomorrow," the officer said.

Rafiq didn't respond; then, a young officer escorted him to a temporary basement cell, which already held an inmate, a black man who continued to sleep undisturbed even when the officer clanged the steel door open. The officer woke the man up and moved him out of the cell into an adjoining one.

He turned to Rafiq and said, "For your safety, you'll be here by your-self; you can bomb us all to hell, but we're supposed to protect you." Then he walked away, whistling to himself.

The room was small and smelled of pungent disinfectant and body odour. Rafiq sat down on the bed. He was exhausted, but his mind was alert. He got up and paced the cell. He could hear the sound of snoring coming from the adjoining cell. It was rhythmic, with a distinct pat-tern—three short bursts followed by a thunderclap. Rafiq got into bed and tried to sleep but his mind was in overdrive. He tossed and turned, finally gave up trying. He went over in his mind the evening's events.

When Ziram informed him, rather harshly, about the family's dis-covery of the emails on his computer, his immediate thought was: how typically Indian in their disregard of privacy. For a few days he had been contemplating confessing to his parents about his involvement with Ahmed Saab ("Saab" out of traditional respect), but he couldn't decide exactly how to do it, and when. When Ziram called, he also felt a little relief that his secret was finally out. On his way home, he had decided to tell them everything—but he changed his mind when he saw Ravindar. He was frightened. A cop was waiting for him. His fear turned to anger and defiance. To him, Ravindar represented the white Canadian establishment—one that oppressed Muslims in Canada, and across the world.

Rafiq wanted to explain to his parents how he had become involved with Ghani Ahmed, and how he wasn't a part of the group and their plans any more. He had been exchanging emails with Ghani Ahmed since late 2004. He had met him once in 2006. But it was more than a year now since he had been in contact with the man. Ghani Ahmed had stopped writing after Rafiq stated his objection to Ahmed's plan, saying clearly that he did not believe that bombing public places and killing innocent people was the answer to the grievances of Muslims. That was early last year.

Rafiq had hoped that Ghani Ahmed would ultimately abandon his murderous schemes. He had planned to tell his parents about his involvement soon after breaking up with the group, but couldn't bring himself to do so, expecting a showdown, an emotional storm at home when he made his confession. His parents had a deeply moral sense and would be irredeemably hurt. He kept postponing the confrontation.

Rafiq was convinced that he had done nothing wrong. But he realized with growing apprehension that the law might see things differently. He had exchanged dozens of emails with Ghani Ahmed. He had been told about the plot to bomb public places in Toronto, and he had scouted places and downloaded maps for Ghani Ahmed. He did reject the plot and moved away from the group—but who would believe him?

He had no idea what to do. Lying on the bed, staring at the ceiling, counting the inevitable beats of the snoring coming from the adjoining cell, he recalled the shock on his parents' faces, his father's anguish and his mother close to breakdown, and he thought how Ziram now had yet another reason to complain about how unfair her life was. His family had struggled for many years in Canada, and he had ruined their lives forever.

They turned poor overnight when they left for Canada, losing the simple comforts they were used to in Bombay. They had lived in an apartment complex crowded with immigrants in northwest Toronto for eleven years, finally purchasing their own place, a townhouse in Mississauga, only after Ziram and he had grown up and had their own jobs, so they could assist with the mortgage payments. They had all hated their apartment. Abba called the building "a vertical slum," and after 9/11, "poor people's Twin Towers." The white neighbourhood contemptuously called the buildings "Paki Palaces."

Even as his heart ached for them, Rafiq couldn't help reflecting how his parents had led a pointless, mechanical life. They were misfits in Canada as much as they had been, as Muslims, in India. Their link to Canada was tenuous, and their link to their native India was fraught with pain. Everything that happened in India still concerned them. He remembered their strained faces when they spoke about the violence between Hindus and Muslims in India, and their utter horror when Muslims were massacred in 2002 during the Gujarat violence.

"It brings back memories of our own loss," Ammi had said.

Abba, more candid than he usually permitted himself to be, responded: "In India, every decade or so, there will be at least one major riot where Muslims are butchered." Then he quietly added, turning to Rafiq, "We came here because we didn't want Ziram and you to go through the constant trauma of that knowledge."

Yet, inexplicably, Abba remained unflinching in his secular, liberal beliefs. The son was convinced that the father lived in the past, clinging to outmoded ideas of respect and tolerance. On the few occasions when they argued over these issues, Rafiq had insisted that Abba's beliefs had become irrelevant after the events of 9/11, and that in the face of persistent persecution Muslims had no choice but to retaliate.

Rafiq knew his values and beliefs had been shaped by his circumstances, not by his upbringing, because he didn't share any of the woolly-headed ideas of his parents, especially those of his Abba. Their beliefs upset him, and what upset him more was that Ammi followed Abba's beliefs without question. Abba had been born a Muslim, and he didn't eat pork or drink alcohol, but that was all there was to his religion. He never went to mosque, prayed, fasted, or read the Quran. But Ammi was a "namaazi," a devout and practising believer who prayed five times a day without fail.

But he loved them and, paradoxically, admired them. Abba had valiantly tried to give his family a life of dignity. He had worked hard in Canada, always looking tired in the morning when he left for work, and tired when he returned in the evening. He did his share of household chores, and often fell into exhausted sleep while sitting down after dinner. Ammi had become more observant in Canada, praying regularly, and praying for miracles. They had both been eager to forget their past and start a new life, but were frustrated because they couldn't find jobs that reflected their abilities. The meagre savings they had brought from India soon dried up, and it was through sheer luck that Abba found his job at the auto parts shop.

Ammi's love was warm, but it couldn't pay for food or clothes. She did minimum-wage survival jobs whenever she could find them, and brought in some spare cash as a seamstress, doing alterations on her sewing machine. Later, when they admitted to themselves that it was impossible to run the family on one meagre income, Ammi reluctantly became a security guard. The kids had to adjust to being home alone. Ziram was old enough but Rafiq wasn't. Luckily they found out about Nagma Khala's crèche in the adjacent tower.

Nagma Khala changed Rafiq's life. Younger than his mother, this honorary aunt lived austerely. There was little to distinguish between Nagma Khala's crèche and Rafiq's home—both were one-bedroom apartments, and both smelled of Indian spices and cooking. She also had a used TV and video player for watching pirated Bollywood movies, of which she was as fond as Ruksana was. Her crèche reflected her life. There was nothing else in the living room except two mattresses along the walls, with long narrow bolsters as backrests. The children ate, played, studied, slept, and prayed in this room every day after school. They learned a bit of Hindustani spoken in the Dakhani dialect. The apartment was on the ground level. Its main door was usually open, except during winter. The screen door was shut at all times, but its glass panel revealed everything inside.

Nagma Khala knew the language of love and caring. With a complexion like dark chocolate, she had light brown eyes, an aquiline nose, thin, pale lips and a deep nasal voice. She covered her head with a dupatta, except when she was with the children; then she allowed herself the luxury of sitting with her head uncovered, revealing her long, neatly braided hair, which was turning grey at the roots.

Nagma had immigrated to Canada from Hyderabad in India after her marriage. Her husband had worked in Muscat before coming to Toronto. In the mid-1980s he had returned to the Middle East to work for an Islamic charity to coordinate aid to war-ravaged Afghanistan, but after some years he had stopped communicating, and the neighbours told Nagma that he probably had started another family where he was.

The neighbours were gossipy, but they were also big-hearted and took care of Nagma's basic needs by giving her free groceries and used clothes. She for her part devoted herself to helping the local Muslim families by looking after their children and teaching them about Islam. Not a trained religious teacher, she used her own methods, telling stories from the Quran and about the goodness of the Prophet and the heroes of Islam. In her living room, Rafiq sat engrossed listening to her stories and explanations.

Someone might ask, "Why should we pray?"

"We must pray because it helps us become better people," was her answer.

"Why five times?"

"We must pray five times because the Prophet said all good Muslims should."

"What if I tell a lie about that and nobody knows?"

"Allah would know."

"What if I have to lie for a good cause?"

"A lie diminishes a good cause."

Rafiq came home every day filled with stories and simple moral teachings and would tell them to his mother. One particular story he remembered vividly. It was about how the Prophet Muhammad cut the sleeve of his robe so that his cat Muezza could sleep while he prayed. Rafiq grew up adoring the Prophet—the messenger of Allah, the perfect human being.

He became Nagma Khala's favourite ward, which made Ruksana jealous occasionally. Nagma Khala took care of Rafiq when he took ill, feeding him warm dal, lentil soup; she would wipe his nose for him. She listened to him when he spoke, helped him form ideas and understand his faith, and thus form an identity. Every time the children quarrelled, she admonished them that violence had no place in Islam, and that even talking harshly to each other was violence. Her message was simple and she often repeated it to them: Allah's path is not easy, but it isn't difficult for the true believer.

Nagma Khala slept on one of the mattresses in the living room. The bedroom didn't have a bed, but it had a computer table and chairs; the community had donated a used desktop computer, which the children learned to use by themselves. A wooden bookshelf nailed on the wall above the computer monitor had a few books on Islam, and a worn copy of the Quran. The computer drew Rafiq to Nagma Khala's place even on weekends.

At first, Rafiq had found it intimidating, but after trying it out and with practice he became good at it. To avoid quarrels with other kids while at Nagma Khala's crèche, he stayed late so he could get more time with the computer. Ruksana would then pick him up after work. By the time he was in his teens, he would be sitting for hours browsing on the internet, reading about Islam.

It was quite by accident that he got into a particular internet chat room. Scrolling through a website that gave guidance about Islam, he saw a "Join the Chat" link blinking alluringly in green and gold. He clicked on it, and discovered strangely named chat buddies hotly debating Islamic issues. He wasn't sure how to join, but once he started, there was no stopping him. He adopted "Gentle One" as his online name; it was another meaning of his name in Arabic, and the one that he preferred, more than the usual "Friend." He had never been able to make friends—the chat room changed all that: he was looking to make just a few but he ended up making many. They were not really friends but acquaintances, and they shared his belief in the purity of Islam, his ideas and ideals, and his anger and anxieties.

He remembered Nagma Khala's stern warning against playing games on the computer. Once, he had chanced upon a gaming site and enthusiastically started to play, but before he could get seriously involved, Nagma Khala was there, admonishing him.

"Playing games on the computer is just one step away from gambling, and you know Islam abhors gambling," she told him.

For Rafiq, that was enough, he never again played games on the computer, although later he became hooked on his Game Boy, and the PSP became a constant companion for many years, until he started working at Wanderlust.

—∞—

The rattling of a prison officer's baton on the steel railings of the cell woke him up abruptly the next morning.

"Up, up, up . . . it is time to get up," the officer shouted in a Caribbean accent, as he ordered everyone out of the cells.

Rafiq nodded at the officer, and followed him down the corridor to a cafeteria for a rudimentary breakfast of a plain bagel and coffee. He was taken to the office of a superintendent, who was seated behind a large desk in a small room. His pink face seemed to balloon out of his shirt, and his rimless glasses and clipped black moustache appeared utterly incongruous to the rest of him.

"You're going to court," he said.

"Will I meet my family?" Rafiq asked.

The superintendent nodded indifferently.

Three

Following Rafiq's arrest and departure with the police, the living room became still. Shortly afterwards Harminder motioned to her husband, Kartar, and the two of them stood up to leave.

"We will come back tomorrow morning," Harminder said, and hugged Ruksana.

Kartar apologized to Abdul. "Sorry, yaar . . . "

"It isn't your fault," Abdul said, waving his hand.

"It is only our fate," Ruksana said.

When they'd gone, Abdul asked Jameel to try Anita's number again, but again there was no answer.

"Perhaps you can try later at night."

"Yes, I'll do that," Jameel said. He was ready to leave but Ziram was too tired to go back to their apartment. She asked him whether they could sleep over, and he nodded.

"We'll stay overnight and sleep in the basement," Ziram said. Her mother's eyes lit up.

"Call us when you speak to the lawyer," Abdul reminded them and went upstairs.

In the bedroom, Ruksana sat on the bed, pulled out a copy of the Quran from the beneath her pillow, and started to read the Arabic verses to calm her nerves. She couldn't focus. So many questions swirled in her mind. What must Rafiq be going through in prison? What kind of questions were the police asking him? He couldn't possibly have slept, could he? Her own flesh, she knew each and every expression on his face, each change of mood. She should have given him his copy of Quran in English. When would she see him? Surely, getting permission to see someone in prison wasn't impossible—but she also knew that Abdul wouldn't have a clue how to go about it. She looked at him, as he sat impassively by the window in his red armchair, lost in thought. She knew better than to prod him with questions.

In the basement, Ziram was worried, too, for Rafiq, and for her parents. But both she and Jameel were also worried about themselves—what fallout would this sudden turn of events have on their lives? Jameel was in line for promotion, and Rafiq's arrest could impact his promotion prospect and perhaps eventually his career, too. They were also worried about Ziram's pregnancy. She moved closer to Jameel, and he held her. She played with the hair on his chest, curling it around with her finger, feeling his warm breath on her forehead.

Recently, Jameel had applied for a deputy director's post at the social services centre where he worked, and he had been shortlisted for the final interview. It was generally agreed at his workplace that Jameel was the best internal candidate. But what would happen now? They were not sure.

"Rafiq's arrest will affect the promotion," Ziram whispered.

"It's possible."

"But why should they hold it against you? You've done nothing wrong."

"I've to work in the community, and the community won't take such things lightly. If people are unwilling to interact with me for whatever reason, the centre's work will suffer."

"You're better known in the community."

"That's true, but right now that's a bit of a problem because everyone will also know about Rafiq."

"What if they select someone else?"

"I'll have to look for another opportunity when all this dies down. For now, we'll have to adjust."

"Abba and Ammi aren't going to be able to handle all this. Did you see their faces, and how they were holding each other when they climbed up the stairs? It was like they needed each other's support. I've never seen them like that."

"That's easy to understand. I'd be devastated to know my son's a—" Jameel began, but then stopped. He didn't want to call Rafiq a terrorist.

"Rafiq screwed up his life, we're not responsible, so why should we have to suffer the consequences," Ziram said angrily.

"Don't talk like that in their presence," Jameel replied and turned around on the bed. He was tired and wanted to sleep. Just when he started to breathe deeply, his cellphone rang. He woke up with a groan. It was Anita. He should have guessed. Anita and he had worked together many years ago when she was still a law student, and they had continued to have a great rapport. She had gone on to become a human rights lawyer. He told her what had happened at his in-laws' home that evening. He also told her that Ravindar had said that the crown would seek his remand.

"That's routine," Anita said.

"Can we move a bail plea then?"

He gestured to Ziram to call her parents. She shook her head.

"Sure, that's possible," Anita said. "But in such circumstances bail isn't granted automatically. The court allows time for investigation. If he's booked under terror charges, there'll be a special hearing. That's when you can make the bail plea."

"When does that happen?"

"In about a week or so."

"But then who'll represent Rafiq at the remand hearing?" Jameel asked.

"The Duty Counsel."

"Can the family attend the remand hearing tomorrow?"

"Yes, that's open to the public. Why don't I meet the family at two tomorrow in my office."

Jameel hung up, and Ziram said she would tell her parents about the lawyer first thing in the morning. He went to sleep immediately. Ziram was too wound up, and she sat up in bed worrying.

"I'm not going to let him ruin our life," she muttered to herself. "He is not my responsibility."

She had to make that clear to her parents, but she knew perfectly well she wouldn't be able to. She got up and rummaged through Rafiq's bookshelf. She pulled out one from a stack next to his table that he had piled on their sides. It had a green cover with gold letters: *My Dream*, by

Ghani Ahmed. She opened it quickly. Ghani Ahmed had signed it. "To Rafiq, marching together for a just cause."

She flipped through the first few pages.

> My dream is a project. I believe that dreams are a sign from Allah of what should be. Every human being must fulfil his or her dream. But we must all make a distinction between a dream and a desire. Desires are concealed wants. Desires are not rooted in reality. Desires are profane. Desires tend to be emotionally destructive. On the other hand, dreams are ambitions. If the dreams of all human beings were to be fulfilled or achieved, our world will become more liveable and just.

Ziram flipped through a few more pages.

> . . . the battle will be lost if the people who struggle for the holy war will focus on the external manifestation of victory. These are Western concepts. I want my dreamers to first focus on internal victory. When a dreamer does that, he realizes that victory and defeat are merely two sides of a duality that forms a part of any human situation and is not specific to a battle.

"What fucking crap," Ziram muttered, and turned a few more pages.

> . . . innocent blood is spilt. The dreamer is not directly responsible for the deaths of these innocent people. He will feel extreme remorse at having been the cause of death of

> so many people unknown to him. That
> remorse is natural. If the dreamer
> doesn't feel so, he is not fit to be a
> martyr. He is a butcher. I don't want
> such human beings to be a part of my
> mission. My dreamers are not killers.
> My dreamers are soft-spoken men who
> are pained to see injustice of any
> form in the world.

She shook Jameel's arm to wake him up.

"What?" he groaned, sitting up annoyed.

"Get up, read this book."

"What time is it?" he rubbed his eyes to adjust to the light and looked at his watch.

"I don't know, maybe five . . . get up and read this. I have found Rafiq's inspiration. He thinks that being a terrorist is being a dreamer."

"Everyone here is crazy," Jameel said and sat up.

"Oh yeah? Consider yourself fortunate, only a crazy woman like me would've married a loser like you," she said, and gave him the book. She switched on the overhead light. Jameel looked at the book.

"What's the book about?" he said loudly, then dropped his voice.

"Garbage. What's the phrase you use? Yes, drivel and balderdash. Rafiq is an idiot to be brainwashed by such rubbish."

"Ziram please let me sleep."

"I can't sleep."

Jameel tried to read, but couldn't and groaned. He dropped the book and again turned his back to her. She leafed through some more pages. She pulled her laptop out of the bag and Googled Ghani Ahmed. There were many Ghani Ahmeds. She checked the book and saw that Muslims in North America (MINA) was the publisher.

She checked its website. It was down. She checked the cached site. Ghani Ahmed was listed as a mentor. The site was meant for young people who wanted to follow an "uncompromising path to adhere to Islam in an alien environment." It had several sections on a horizontal bar—webcast, news, a section on Quran teachings. The news section had links to Afghanistan, Iraq, Palestine, Kashmir, and Chechnya. There was a separate section on North America, Europe, Israel, and India.

Ziram glanced through the cached home page:

> Our fight is not merely to drive them out of our homelands. Our fight is to establish Islam everywhere.
>
> Struggle is obligatory even if you dislike it.
>
> You must not think that those who were slain in the cause of Allah are dead. They are alive, and well-provided for by their Lord.
>
> Slay them wherever you find them and drive them out of the places where they drove you out from, for persecution is worse than slaughter.

This was zealotry. Fanaticism. She had heard such words uttered in hushed tones by some of their neighbours in the apartment building in which they had lived previously. Abba had cautioned Rafiq and Ziram not to be swayed by such talk.

"Only insecure people preach violence, Islam doesn't," he had said, repeatedly.

She found it hard to believe that Rafiq had turned into a fanatic, but wasn't entirely surprised. Now she blamed her parents for her brother's fanaticism. They were wrong in constantly pampering him to an extent where he had finally lost all sense of proportion. Rafiq's religious rigidity should have become evident to Ammi and Abba, but Ammi chose to call it piety, and Abba, while clearly uncomfortable with Rafiq's increasing religiosity, blamed Nagma Khala for it.

"That woman is making it hard for him to adjust to Canada," he had declared when Ziram told him about Rafiq's near isolation in their building as well as at school. She knew Abba was only partially right,

Nagma Khala was narrow-minded but so were they, and she wasn't evil. This Ghani Ahmed clearly was evil.

From the time she was a child, she had had mixed feelings about her brother. She was protective and indignant at the same time. She leaped to his defence if anyone at school or in the building bullied him, but she also resented the special treatment he received from their parents.

"He is young," her mother always reprimanded her when she complained.

"Just a year younger than me!"

But they continued to indulge him—a larger helping of the sheer-khurma on Eid, or the extra pocket money, which Ammi slipped him on the sly. And Ziram was expected to adjust, be less demanding, more understanding. Ziram had become increasingly frustrated. To keep peace at home she had to ignore her own interests. She had to live with a double standard. She was encouraged to express her opinions on everything, even when these were at variance with what her parents believed. She was raised to become an independent woman, to defend her rights. But they wouldn't let her say anything about her brother, even to acknowledge their bias!

"Abba, he can't make friends—and on the rare occasions when he does, he is not able to keep them," she had said, and suggested that they take Rafiq to a psychiatrist. But her dad had dismissed the idea. "Only white people go to psychiatrists," he said.

And yet, despite all her resentments, she loved Rafiq. The warmest memories she had were of playing with her little brother at home, when they were on their own, or on rare occasions under Ammi's indulgent gaze or Abba's indifferent presence. There were a million such shared moments. She remembered how, after they had moved to Toronto, she took him around and introduced him to the kids in the building. They couldn't follow what the other kids said because of their local Canadian accents, and the kids couldn't understand Ziram and Rafiq because of their Indian accents.

"Try to speak slowly," she advised him. "They don't understand you because you speak fast."

He needed constant attention both at school and at home. During his first week at school she had to look after him because he refused to use the boys' room.

"It is dirty. I can't go in there because there is no tap or water."

"I will come with you."

He had entered the washroom reluctantly, while she waited outside and spoke to him loudly, much to the amusement of the other boys. She rebuked them with sharp words: "We are new here, and my brother is young!"

They both learned to integrate into their new environment, often by watching other kids and sharing with each other what they had observed. Rafiq was the first to catch on to the peculiar lilt in which the kids spoke at school, and taught her not to separate each word while speaking and writing.

"The Canadian way is *it's*, not *it is*," he told her.

—⁓—

She was angry that Rafiq had remained silent with Ravindar, who had come to assist them. To Ziram, Rafiq's silence implied complicity. He should have explained the presence of those emails in his account. She seethed at his sulky attitude; he had jeopardized their lives. She and Jameel had planned to move into a townhouse in time for the newborn to arrive. Their plans were based on Jameel's promotion. Now all that was up in the air because of her idiot brother's recklessness.

Ziram felt resentment at her parents too, because they would now expect her to help Rafiq. She also knew that she couldn't really escape her responsibility, however burdensome; they had nobody else to turn to, and she wasn't going to abandon them. Her happiness was meaningless without their happiness. In what seemed an utterly hopeless situation, she knew she could depend upon Jameel, because he understood; he would stand by her.

Four

When she came up to make breakfast for Jameel, Ziram found that her mother had dozed off at the dining table. Ammi got up early to pray, and she usually took the opportunity to nod off whenever she could. Ziram sat down quietly on a chair beside her mother, and gazed at her lovingly; gently, she ran her fingers through her mother's hair. Ruksana opened her eyes and raised her head. She smiled a tired smile, stifled a yawn with her palm. Ammi was so graceful, and though she pretended otherwise, she cared about how she looked—even at home. The daughter often teased the mother that she was "carefully careless."

"Why don't you use hair colour instead of putting on henna?" Ziram would ask. Henna gave Ruksana's hair a red-brown colour that was coarse and also too obvious and traditional. She had asked the question often enough, but Ammi never answered. But Ziram knew the answer—her mother wanted to look young, but not too much younger than Abba.

"Why are you up so early?" Ruksana asked.

"I didn't sleep at all, but forget that. Jameel's lawyer friend asked us to meet her this afternoon."

Ruksana sat up. "What else did she say? Does Saabji know?"

"No, I wanted to talk to you first. I'm never sure of Abba's reaction to anything."

"Did she say anything about bail?"

"He can't get bail right now, but maybe after ten days or some such thing. Jameel spoke to her. You ask him."

"I hope Jameel comes up before your father comes down."

"I'll make breakfast for him," Ziram said. "He's going to work. I'll stay here."

At her parent's place, Ziram had to cook for Jameel, because he found Ruksana's cooking too greasy. But she found cooking even a simple breakfast in her mother's kitchen intimidating—all the steel and chrome there made her feel like she had walked into a sci-fi movie. She was afraid of spoiling her mother's perfectly shining world by inadvertently scratching one of her appliances, although she had bought them all for her mother.

Then, of course, there was another insurmountable problem— Ruksana's home-made condiments and spices. Ziram had no idea how to get the balance right. Ammi ground all her spices instead of buying the stuff ready-made. She believed that this was more economical, and also made her food taste special.

"Ammi, even in your India nobody does these things anymore," Ziram would grumble. But Ruksana continued with her own ways.

Ruksana followed her daughter to the kitchen. "Is it already time for him to go?" she said, looking at the digital clock on the refrigerator. "I was hoping we could talk to him about his lawyer friend and what she can do for us."

Ziram nodded absently. She was wary about talking to Ammi in case she said something about Rafiq that her mother didn't want to hear. But that morning Ruksana was desperate and, clutching at Ziram's arm, she asked plaintively, "What will happen to him?"

"Ammi, don't worry. They won't harm Rafiq. This is Canada, not your India." She gave her mother a light hug.

"I wouldn't be so sure about that," Jameel said, arriving from behind.

They hadn't heard him come to the kitchen. He was already dressed for work, wearing the same clothes he had worn the previous day; he had wanted to iron the shirt but couldn't find the iron.

He had slept fitfully and was annoyed that Ziram had woken him up so early. His eyes were puffy and he desperately needed tea. He didn't like Ruksana's cooking, but loved her tea, or chai, because she made it milky and sweet. She made it in the Bombay style of the Irani cafes. Ruksana sat down and faced him; she knew that Jameel wouldn't evade her questions. Ziram brought him a cup of chai and scrambled eggs.

"Will the lawyer be able to get him out?" Ruksana asked him, her eyes searching his face for clues.

"I don't know."

"Why can't she accept the case right away and apply for bail today?"

"Yes Jameel, why don't you ask Anita once again, maybe she'll agree now?" Ziram said.

Jameel called Anita; she was just leaving for work and sounded in a hurry.

"Can't you accept the case, and come to the court for the hearing?" Jameel asked her.

"Jameel, I know how the family must be feeling, but there's nothing I can do right now. I must know the details of the case. I don't know anything more than what you told me yesterday. Besides, there's really no point in moving the bail today because, as I said yesterday, it most likely won't be granted."

"So, what do we do today?"

"Tell the Duty Counsel not to move for bail; we will study the case, and then move for bail a few days later."

Jameel told Ruksana what Anita suggested.

"Can't we do anything today?" Ruksana asked again. "Allah alone knows what will happen. I hope they don't torture him, you hear such horrible things nowadays. Can't we at least go to the court to see him?"

Jameel looked at Ziram.

"Of course, we'll go," she said.

After Jameel left for work, Ruksana told Ziram to go upstairs and wake her father. "We must get ready quickly. And when we meet the lawyer, you talk to her. Your father will ramble on and talk too much."

Ziram smiled. Ammi was uncomfortably sharp in her observations, but always accurate. Soon they heard Abba's peculiar gargling noise coming down from the washroom upstairs. Abdul had been a reluctant user of mouthwash, he had started using it only when his steel tongue-cleaner from India broke. Now he was hooked to it, using the mouth-wash several times a day. When he came down, Ziram told him that they had spoken to Anita.

"We should go to his remand hearing," Ruksana added. "From there, we will go to meet the lawyer, so wear proper clothes, and let Ziram do the talking."

"Why? She won't charge us if we wear good clothes?" Abdul said sarcastically. "Anyway, we must fix a time to meet Rafiq in the jail. Let us find out from Ravindar."

He stopped in his tracks when Ruksana shouted, "You will not talk to that man ever again!" Her eyes were flashing.

"All right," he replied wearily.

—⁓—

As they were about to depart for the Brampton courthouse, Ruksana hurried down to the basement and pulled out Rafiq's copy of the Quran in English. He would need it. She came out of the house looking determined. Abdul and Ziram watched her with some awe; it was at such times that she could be a pillar of strength.

Ziram drove the three of them, taking local roads to avoid the morning traffic. They parked the car in the sprawling lot, then walked past a well-manicured lush green lawn to reach the large grey, concrete building of the courthouse. It looked intimidating. At the entrance hall they went through a metal detector and were frisked.

They looked around them in silence. The place was busy. Lawyers in black jackets and starched white collars, carrying or pulling at briefcases on wheels; ordinary citizens like themselves, looking lost; a noisy camera crew. At the information desk they awaited their turn and were told where to go. Following the instructions, they took an elevator up, but had difficulty locating their designated courtroom. As they asked around, they saw Ravindar. He greeted them cordially; Abdul and Ziram acknowledged him politely, Ruksana gave him an icy stare.

"Let me take you there," Ravindar offered and led them down the corridor. "I'm sorry about what happened last evening," he said. "I had to report the incident to my superiors, and I had no control over what happened afterwards." He paused, expecting them to say something, but they didn't.

"Have you hired a lawyer?" he asked.

"Anita Persaud," Ziram said. "My husband knows her; but she isn't coming for the remand hearing."

They arrived at the courtroom. It was almost empty, except for a Duty Counsel, who was a woman, a few police officers, and another woman, who looked like an attorney. Abdul and Ziram exchanged greetings with the Duty Counsel. Ziram told her that their lawyer Anita Persaud would move for bail later.

Ruksana gave a gasp as Rafiq entered the courtroom, escorted by a policeman. He looked dishevelled, wearing the same clothes in which they had last seen him. She fought back her tears, while the others could only stare at him pitifully. He couldn't meet their eyes.

The officials went about their business. It was routine for them. The crown attorney sought a remand based on the evidence the police had gathered. He claimed that Rafiq belonged to an Islamist group that had planned serial bombings across Toronto on New Year's Eve in 2008. Several young men were involved in the conspiracy, he said, and one Ghani Ahmed, the kingpin, was still at large. The Justice of the Peace granted a week's remand.

Rafiq remained expressionless, and just before he was taken away, his parents rushed forward to him. Abdul and Ruksana embraced him.

"Ammi, Abba, this isn't true," he said. He now seemed crushed by his situation. "I tried to save lives. Get me a lawyer, I've nothing to hide."

"We are meeting a lawyer later today," Abdul told him, "Why didn't you say anything yesterday? Why didn't you explain . . . ?"

"I was scared first, and then angry that you called a cop before you spoke to me. I didn't want to talk in his presence."

"We will come to meet you tomorrow," Ruksana said hurriedly, and gave him his English Quran as the police led him away. "Pray all the time, and read from the holy book, it will bring you peace of mind." Rafiq took the Quran and walked away with his escort. Ghani Ahmed had given it to him.

Ravindar informed them that Rafiq would be taken to the Maplehurst detention centre. "You can meet him two times a week, twenty minutes on each visit."

Abdul and Ruksana were distraught, looked at each other in despair. Abdul gave a shrug and turned away hopelessly, Ruksana turned her eyes upwards. Ziram embraced her mother tightly, and gripped her father's shoulder to support him. He looked at her and nodded his thanks.

"You're doing just fine," Ziram told Ruksana. "Not breaking down in his presence. That's courageous."

From the Brampton courthouse, she drove them to Yonge and Sheppard in Toronto for their meeting with Anita. The lawyer was a short, dark-skinned woman, in her mid-thirties, with close-cropped, jet-black hair. She wore a short black skirt and a white shirt. Despite this formal attire, she was friendly. She smiled warmly at Ruksana and shook her hand. Then she shook hands with Abdul and Ziram. Her office was overflowing with files and papers, on her table and on the shelves. A wheeled carry-on beside her table was stacked with more papers. Her jacket hung on the back of her chair.

"We want you to represent our son," Abdul said to her.

"Before that, let me first understand the case," Anita replied, in a matter-of-fact manner.

Ignoring Ruksana's instructions to let Ziram do the talking, Abdul narrated all that had happened the previous evening. It came out in a rush. Ziram added some bits and pieces. Anita wanted to know about the family—when they had immigrated to Canada, what they had done in India, how they were occupied in Canada, how the kids had been raised. She took copious notes.

Ruksana said, "Even if he has done wrong, please help my son."

Anita reached across her worktable, and gently patted Ruksana's hand.

"This Ravindar is a bit of a skunk isn't he? But I guess they must've been investigating the case for a while. What do you think was Rafiq's actual involvement with this Ghani Ahmed?"

"We don't really know," Abdul said, and Ruksana nodded in agreement.

"But the evidence is completely circumstantial," Ruksana said.

Abdul gave a little smile, and Anita looked up at Ruksana with renewed interest.

"Do you think he is being framed?" she asked Ruksana.

"That may be possible," Ruksana said, though she didn't sound convincing.

"But how do you explain those emails?"

"Rafiq told us that he has done nothing wrong." Ruksana said this with complete conviction.

Abdul said to Anita, "So, will you take our case?"

Anita nodded. "Yes, I will. I must also talk to him to get a better idea of his involvement," she said.

She deduced that Rafiq's involvement was at best tangential; her assessment was based on what the parents had told her. Having worked as a civil rights lawyer for many years, she was perennially wary and suspicious of the State's interpretation of the law, especially when dealing with minorities. She had seen many cases where innocent people had been falsely implicated. Anita assured them that she would carefully examine the charges against Rafiq, and then talk to him.

She asked them to come in again the next day. Then, looking at Ziram, she said, "If they can't come, we can talk on the phone. Also, be ready for police interrogation. They may want to talk to all of you, and definitely to the parents."

For the first time since their son was led away by the police, Ruksana and Abdul felt relieved, and it showed on their faces. They knew this didn't mean that Rafiq was out of trouble, but it was a good sign. Anita assured them that she would move for bail soon.

"What about your fees?" Abdul said without a trace of embarrassment.

"Don't worry," Anita said, "I'll be reasonable."

Ziram asked Anita about the media's involvement in the case. She didn't say what actually worried her, the adverse impact of the publicity on Jameel's promotion. Ruksana misunderstood her daughter's apprehension and got excited at the suggestion.

"In India, our experience was that if we got the media, we could swing public mood in our favour," she said. Seeing her daughter's frown she added, "But I don't know how it works here."

Anita smiled at Ruksana. "The crown generally seeks a media blackout so that the investigations are conducted without interference," she said. She also cautioned them not to be too optimistic and to be patient. "The provisions of the terrorism laws are quite broad and tricky," she said.

"What do you mean?" Ruksana asked.

"Well, a person could be implicated and arrested for merely being aware of a specific activity of a group—even that could be interpreted as terrorist activity."

"Rafiq told us he was involved only initially," Abdul said impatiently.

"Let me talk to him tomorrow and get all the details," Anita replied.

"When can we meet Rafiq?" Ruksana asked.

"You're allowed two visits a week. You can go tomorrow and meet him. I'll move the papers to be retained his lawyer, and meet him separately."

—⁂—

"She's a West Indian, isn't she?" Ruksana said as they came out of Anita's office.

"*Caribbean,*" Ziram corrected her, amused. "Just like your son-in-law. Guyanese parents, I'd guess. I wonder why she didn't ask us about Jameel."

—⁂—

When Jameel arrived that evening, Abdul was watching TV, Ziram was playing with her cellphone, and Ruksana was in the kitchen making chai. The family appeared calmer, and that most likely meant that their meeting with Anita had gone well.

"How do you know Anita?" Ziram asked.

"We worked together many years back," he said; then he looked sharply at his wife and grinned.

When the phone rang, Ruksana groaned. "Who can it be at this time?" A man's voice at the other end pronounced the greeting, "As salam aleikum."

"Waleikum salam," Ruksana responded, without emotion.

After a brief pause, the man said, "Ahmed Saab has asked me to call you. Do you need anything? Please let me know." He spoke in English.

"Who is it?"

"We are Ghani Ahmed's friends. Is there anything you need?" The caller had switched to Hindustani.

When she heard that name, the phone slipped from Ruksana's hand and fell to the floor. She stood rooted, looking at everyone uncomprehendingly. Ziram picked up the phone.

"Who is it?" she asked.

"We are Ghani Ahmed's friends."

"Please hold." Ziram put her hand over the mouthpiece and called Jameel, who had just sat down beside Abdul to watch TV.

"This guy says he is Ghani Ahmed's friend. Talk to him." Jameel got up.

"Wait!" Abdul shouted, "give me the phone." He lunged for it, stumbling in the process.

"Who are you?" he demanded angrily, his voice rough, rasping in his throat.

"I am Ahmed Saab's friend. If you need anything, please let me know," the man repeated.

"Haramzaade!" Abdul bellowed into the phone. "Bastard, if you are so keen to help us, go tell the cops where that madarchod motherfucker Ghani Ahmed is. Don't call us again." He collapsed into his chair, wheezing for breath.

The family stared at him, stunned. Ruksana rushed to him and put her hand on his arm. "Ziram, get water for Saabji . . . quickly." When she offered him the glass, he waved her away.

"Saabji, have some water, you will feel better," Ruksana said, her voice a mix of plea and command.

"Abba, take it easy," Ziram said.

"Let us make him lie down," Ruksana said. Abdul again waved her away.

"Saabji, come lie down on the couch. What if you get another heart attack?"

Reluctantly, and with great effort, Abdul got up. Ziram and Jameel helped him to the couch. Ruksana sat on the carpet and massaged his chest as he lay down. Ziram sat at his feet, massaging his legs.

"Go and get Kartar and Harminder," Ruksana told Jameel.

"No, I'm OK," Abdul whispered. His face was now drained, his lips were dry and quivering.

Abdul had hoped that perhaps Rafiq wasn't really involved in the terror plot, that it had all been some sort of elaborate mistake that would eventually be sorted out. But the phone call from Ghani Ahmed's friend had finally crushed that hope.

"We should inform Anita and Ravindar," Ziram suggested.

Ruksana was furious. "Absolutely not. Nobody talks to Ravindar. Saabji you talk to the lawyer tomorrow."

Jameel checked the phone for the caller's ID, but it was unlisted. He exchanged a look with Ziram, and then switched on the TV again. The weather forecast said that it was going to be a cold November night.

Ruksana whispered to Abdul to ask Jameel to stay. Abdul knew that Ruksana needed Ziram, and that Ziram wouldn't stay without Jameel.

"Beta Jameel, please stay with us tonight," he said. "I don't think we can manage by ourselves."

"Of course, I'm here for you," Jameel replied affably, without pausing to think.

His father-in-law clutched his hand hard in gratitude. Abdul's shoulders started to shake slightly; then the tremor began to spread, slowly and with increasing urgency; he started to sob, in fits at first, and then loudly, giving great shuddering sobs. He had been stoic and silent, now the dam in his heart had finally burst. It was the wrenching cry of a man who felt hopeless, desperate, betrayed. Ruksana asked Ziram and Jameel to help her take Abdul to the bedroom.

—⁂—

Ruksana wanted to offer the evening namaaz before going to bed. Abdul lay on the bed looking sullen. She knew that it was better to keep quiet during such moods.

"All this wouldn't have happened if you had been strict with him," Abdul said.

She was on her prayer rug, about to start her namaaz. She knew what was to follow. He would rant about her "relationship" with Dhinmant, the trade union leader who had been her saviour and mentor, and was killed in Bombay during the 1992-93 religious violence.

"When they were growing up, you were busy with Dhinmant. You had no time for them," he muttered.

Ruksana had heard all this before—harsher accusations even—and was no longer disturbed by it. She knew better than to get into an endless, unwinnable argument. She quietly completed her prayer, turned briefly to Abdul, and said softly, "Saabji, you need rest. We all need rest."

Five

Abdul and Ruksana slept at different times. She went to sleep and woke up early. She got up twice every night—at around 2:00 a.m. to use the washroom, and then at 4:00 a.m. to pray and read from her holy book. Abdul stayed up late and went to bed just before dawn, when Ruksana's day began. When he was younger, Abdul read newspapers late into the night. In Canada, however, newspapers became a luxury, and watching TV replaced reading. Sometimes Abdul flipped through the community newspapers that Kartar brought from his shop, but they irritated him because they were so amateurish and full of vulgar advertisements. That night, sleep eluded Ruksana, and after tossing and turning for some time she sat up. Abdul, too, was in no hurry to go to sleep; he sat on his red armchair instead, gazing out of the window at the dark sky and the distant stars.

Ruksana took her prayer rug and her Quran and went down to the kitchen. Before offering the namaaz, she performed her ablutions: she washed her hands up to the wrists, cleansed her mouth, rinsed her nostrils, washed her face, poured water over both her arms—right arm first and then the left—touched her forehead with her wet hand and wet her ears. She poured water on her feet up to her ankles. She did all this three times. After the ablution, she looked at herself in the mirror. Usually she would sigh and swiftly turn away. Today she continued to stare at her puffy eyes, and the pouches beneath them. Her forehead seemed to have more lines than the previous morning.

Prayer was her moment to be with herself, and with Allah—to be at peace and to contemplate. It gave her comfort and strength to face the world. She preferred to pray in the kitchen because it was her own private space. When work kept her out of the home, she found time to pray at dawn and in the evening. Ruksana never asked anything from Allah—but today she couldn't control herself.

"Ya Allah! Haven't I suffered enough? Take me away and stop my pain . . . "

—⁓—

The twists and turns that her life had taken still never failed to bewilder her. Now just when they were all finally settling down in Canada, everything had come crashing down around them again. When they bought the townhouse, Abdul had insisted on calling it Manzil, or Destination. She had liked the name too. This house was their final aspiration and their destiny. The kids simply called it home. They often found their parents' misty-eyed nostalgia for everything Indian embarrassing and irritating.

Except for the name, which gave it some sort of distinct identity, there was nothing else distinctive about the house. It had the usual layout: kitchen, dining room, and living room on the main level, and two bedrooms with a washroom on the floor above. The backyard was small and barren despite Ruksana's valiant attempts at greening it. They ignored it in the winter and used it to dry clothes in the summer. There was a decent front lawn, with which Ruksana struggled, trying to keep it trim and growing flowers.

Abdul and Ruksana were keen to lease out the basement to supplement the mortgage payments, but Rafiq wouldn't let them. He had never had a room for himself, and his small bedroom upstairs wasn't enough. After much argument, Ruksana agreed to let him have the basement if he let her keep her washing machine there. He utilized his salary from his new job at Wanderlust to fill the basement with furniture—an oversize TV, a couch, a treadmill, a worktable, which was now stacked with audio and video CDs about Islamic teachings, web-design manuals, and brochures, and a shelf where he kept his religious books.

Ruksana deployed Ziram's salary to turn the kitchen into a steel-and-chrome citadel. Everything in the kitchen was made of stainless steel—pots, pans, electric range, dishwasher, and microwave oven. A two-door refrigerator occupied prime place against one wall. A "Made in India" food processor, for which Ziram paid a ransom to an appliance store in Brampton, was kept safely in a steel-door cabinet and came out only on the special occasions when Ruksana made biryani. Later, Ziram installed a hood over the kitchen range to dispel cooking odours, but Ruksana seldom used it because "it makes a lot of noise" and, she argued, "What is wrong with curry smell?" Abdul called the kitchen "Ruksana's showroom" because she didn't use nearly half the gadgets.

—⁓—

After being alone for a while in the bedroom, Abdul went downstairs and sat beside Ruksana on the kitchen floor. His creaky joints made this simple task seem excruciating. Getting up was even more difficult. Years of neglecting his health had aged him prematurely. Generally, he had little patience with his wife's religiosity. His own belief in the benevolent almighty was tenuous, and had been so since his mother's death from tuberculosis when he was a child. He was convinced that Allah tested only the good folks, leaving the evil ones alone, and was sarcastic about Ruksana's piety. Today, however, he was quiet.

He watched her: so graceful and lithe, wearing her white prayer cape, which covered her from head to waist. She had on his reading glasses. She hated glasses because they made her "look old"; so she didn't have her own pair, but increasingly she found it difficult to read without them.

"Go ask Ziram if they can stay with us for a few days," Ruksana said, her eyes on the book, moving her finger from right to left.

"A little later," he said, and then, irritated, asked her: "How long do you want them to be here?" He was actually annoyed that she wanted him to get up just when he had sat down with such difficulty.

"Saabji, go now."

Even after so many years of being together, or perhaps because of that, they argued about everything and endlessly nagged each other, but Abdul eventually relented, even when he disagreed. Their constant quarrelling was a joke in the family. A couple of months ago in September—during Ramzan—they celebrated both their 25th wedding anniversary and Ziram's pregnancy. To break the fast, Rafiq had organized a surprise iftar party for them at home in the evening. He had also invited their neighbours. Everyone had made jokes about their constant bickering, and they had smiled in embarrassment. The fare had been rice, poriyal, appalam, and pickle: having lived in Bombay, both Abdul and Ruksana loved South Indian cuisine and sorely missed it in Toronto.

Abdul creakily rose and slowly made his way to the basement. He knocked lightly on the door and whispered, "Ziram, your mother wants you to stay here for a few days . . . "

Ziram replied softly, "OK."

He stood by the door for a moment, expecting her to open it, but when she didn't, he slowly climbed up the stairs. Here was a fresh example of how well his wife understood their kids; he never ceased to be amazed at that. He had been diffident about disturbing Ziram, but Ruksana knew their daughter would be awake. He returned to sit beside her. "She will stay," he said. They sat together quietly.

Abdul again recalled the surprise party. Ziram had announced her pregnancy to the family just a few days before, and they were all ecstatic, especially Ruksana, who hadn't stopped smiling ever since she heard that she was to become a grandmother soon. Rafiq had organized the surprise party all by himself. Sitting on the floor with his wife, Abdul reminded himself, with a twinge, that his son must have been involved with Ghani Ahmed even then.

Ruksana usually found her mornings calm and soothing, but today she was uncomfortable. She found Abdul's heavy breathing oppressive. He put his hand on her shoulder, hoping to comfort her. She put a finger on the line she was reading and stopped to look at him; her eyes were moist.

"Saabji, why did Rafiq do this? And why now, when everything was finally working out for us?"

"Naseeb, Ruksana . . . Fate. Our destiny is to suffer." Abdul sighed, moved closer to her, and gently pulled her towards him.

Ruksana put her head on his shoulder and, holding his hand, said, "Everyone has problems; but our problems . . . they change our lives.

Come, you must rest now. And next time don't sit down on the floor, you know you have trouble getting up."

Now she thinks about that, Abdul said to himself, but smiled meekly at her. She stood up, still holding Abdul's hand; he put his other hand on his knee, and slowly stood up. She led him to their bedroom and helped him lie down. Abdul pulled up the comforter and covered himself; within minutes Ruksana heard him snoring softly. She switched off the table lamp and sat by the bed for some moments, lost in her thoughts.

Six

R afiq was taken to Maplehurst detention centre in Milton, a large, forbidding brick structure behind a wire fence, with a few windows looking out. Inside, it looked like a prison as he had always imagined it, with the aid of television. An officer took charge of him at the entrance and escorted him to a windowless room with a table and two chairs. A genial-looking black man with grey hair sat behind the table with a form to fill out. He didn't introduce himself. In a tinny voice, he asked Rafiq to answer the same questions he had been asked at the police station the previous night. Rafiq couldn't hide his restlessness.

The officer ignored his fidgeting and continued methodically to fill out the form. When he was done, he picked up his single sheet of paper and shuffled out of the room. He returned with an orange prison suit for Rafiq. The sight of it sank his heart. Why had he been so cocky the previous night? When he had put it on—it was oversized but comfortably warm—he was led by the officer out and down the corridor to his cell. On the way the man described the place to him as if it were a tourist resort.

"The detention centre can take up to 1500 inmates. The pods are self-contained units where inmates spend their days . . . each pod is made up of six thirty-two-bed units, each with a common area. Each pod also has rooms for interviews, activities, and visitors and a centre yard for getting some fresh air. It's covered partly by a solid roof and partly by wire . . . "

Rafiq wasn't really listening. They were in a clinically clean white corridor, on both sides of which were rooms, some open, others shut. There were showers at the end. In the common area there were chairs and tables scattered about, and there was a TV set in the middle. It was turned on and showing a movie. An aging white prisoner, with a long beard and straggly hair was watching TV. He waved a hand and sang, or rather bellowed, "Welcome to the Milton Hilton. You can check in any time you like but you can never leave." The officer grinned.

Rafiq's cell had a bunk bed, a sink, and a toilet. Pointing to the toilet, the officer said, "This is for everything, showers outside." Then he left. The cell smelled of disinfectant. It was bleak. Rafiq sat on the bed. It had a thin mattress and an itchy woollen blanket. At least the toilet bowl was spotless. He was hungry and itchy, he scratched his beard. He was also eager to talk to the lawyer and tell her his story. He hoped she would understand him. There was so much to explain.

—⁓—

He had believed in Ghani Ahmed's cause and was convinced for a long time that it was just. He had parted ways only because he could not see himself planting bombs to kill people. Massacre of innocent people wouldn't bring any glory to Islam or avenge atrocities against the Muslims, he had argued in his note to Ghani Ahmed. His mentor didn't want to hear this, and had stopped communicating with Rafiq. A year before their email exchanges stopped, his mentor then cajoled him into participating in a religious camp in Kathmandu, Nepal, a journey which resulted in nothing more than spending some time in an idyllic resort; there was no religious camp, there was nobody there except himself. Afterwards he had been taken to Ahmedabad in India, to meet with the families of the Muslim victims of the 2002 religious riots. There, he had fallen ill due to the intense summer heat and had to rush back to Toronto.

Rafiq was determined to tell the lawyer everything, all that he had wanted to tell his parents, but never did or could. Now it was too late. Since his arrest, he hadn't stopped feeling sorry for his parents. Ammi and Abba would never be able to accept the fact of their son having served time in prison for a crime. He didn't particularly care—as yet— about being in prison, but he was worried about its effect on his family. He had destroyed their lives, which they had painstakingly rebuilt after years of hardship and struggle. He was willing to do anything, undergo any punishment, if he could only change that.

Time crawled, each moment an eternity. For many hours, he gazed at the wall or lay down on the bed, and tried unsuccessfully to sleep. He was relieved when an officer finally arrived to escort him to a special room to meet his lawyer. The room was small; there were two reclining chairs, a low wood and glass table, and a rug underneath the table. A window with blinds that were partially drawn let the sunlight in; there were panel lights in the ceiling. Anita smiled when she saw him. She got up, shook his hand. The officer who had escorted Rafiq to the room told Anita that he would be waiting outside. Rafiq was eager to make the right impression on Anita, but to her he seemed distracted and worried.

"Rafiq, you've been charged as a terrorist involved in a bombing conspiracy. This is a serious offence, and you could end up being here for a very long time. So, I need to know all there is to this conspiracy; tell me everything, leave nothing out. Most of the guys from your group have been arrested."

Rafiq looked at her in disbelief.

"I don't know anyone from the group except Ahmed Saab—Ghani Ahmed. I mean, I knew there were others, there had to be, but I swear I didn't know them. I never met them."

"All of them are about your age—eighteen to twenty years old. Do you know where Ghani Ahmed is?"

Rafiq shook his head.

"The Crown Attorney claims that while several sites across Toronto are targeted, the main threat is to Nathan Phillips Square, and that on December 31 a series of explosions has been or had been planned to rip through the place. Is that true?"

Rafiq crossed his arms uneasily. "I don't know. All I know is that everything was set for some time this year."

"The year is not yet over; that means the threat is still real, the explosions may happen?"

"I don't know. I haven't been in touch with him since the middle of last year."

"You've done a certificate program in computers."

"Yes, web design at Sheridan."

"Did you help Ghani Ahmed to create a cyber-nerve centre?"

"I've no idea what that means."

"Did you ever talk to your parents?"

"About what?"

"Your views, your ideas."

"Yes, of course."

"And they agreed with you?"

"Sort of. All Muslims would agree."

"To what?"

"That they are treated badly here."

"And about Ghani Ahmed's plans?"

"No."

"Why not?"

Rafiq didn't answer. He pulled his bare feet out of his sneakers and curled his toes.

"How many times did you meet him?"

"We've mostly exchanged emails for about three years or so. I met him just once, a couple of years ago, at an Indian restaurant in Mississauga when he told me to go to Kathmandu."

"Is he of Indian origin?"

"I think so, South Asian definitely. He sounded like one."

"There were seven sites chosen to hide the bombs?"

"I don't know."

"You sent maps of seven sites?"

"He told me to make detailed maps of seven different places. I downloaded them from Google and sent them to him."

"Which places?"

"Square One, Finch, Eaton Centre, Yorkdale, that Jewish place at Spadina, a temple at Gore Road, and a cathedral in downtown."

"So there were seven sites."

"I was asked to visit each of these places and draw detailed maps. He would then visit them to select the sites."

When Rafiq saw Anita looking at him intensely, he quickly added, "I wasn't involved beyond this stage. I told him—wrote to him—I was against the murder of innocent people. Also, he wanted me to give specific maps with more details. I didn't do that; I just sent him the Google maps, and then we stopped communicating."

"But you did send him the maps, and he sent you the plan."

He nodded.

"Where were the explosives to come from?" Anita asked.

"I don't know," he blurted out, clearly frightened. "I really don't know. I was a part of all this only initially," Rafiq said, looking balefully at Anita.

"There's nothing to show you withdrew, not one email you stored on your computer indicates that."

"I wrote to him that killing innocent people was wrong, and when he didn't reply, I stopped writing to him."

"Help me understand the sequence. What happened after you identified the sites?"

"I didn't identify the sites. I merely sent him maps of seven different places, and in that email, I said I didn't support his plan."

"So what did he say?"

"Nothing. He didn't contact me at all thereafter."

"The cops believe that Ghani Ahmed may still pull something off," she said in a serious tone. "Let's hope he doesn't."

Anita was certain that Rafiq knew more than he was willing to admit or talk.

"About a year before we exchanged these emails about his plans, he had asked me to go to Kathmandu for a religious camp."

"What was this workshop all about?"

"It was a religious camp in Kathmandu, but it was called off."

"Why?"

"I've no idea. Nobody showed up."

"And you were in Kathmandu when you were told of the cancellation?"

"Yes."

"Then?"

"Then I went to Ahmedabad in India."

"What happened there?"

"I was taken to meet Muslims whose family members had been killed during the 2002 riots. Their homes had been destroyed."

"Your passport will show these trips?"

He nodded. "Yes, of course. But believe me, nothing happened."

Rafiq was leaning forward, speaking fast, his voice high. The officer who was standing inside the room moved away from the door and came closer to where Anita and Rafiq were sitting. Rafiq was desperate to convince Anita of his innocence, but he could see that she was nowhere near convinced.

"How did you get involved in all this?" she asked.

"I believe—believed—that Ghani Ahmed was right about what was happening to Muslims in the world."

He was hesitant about discussing his past, but in an hour Anita was able to draw it out from him. She asked him about his school, his friends, how he got along with his parents. It was evident to her that this man-child believed he had done nothing wrong because he was no longer a part of Ghani Ahmed's plan.

"What happens now?"

"I'll move your bail hearing for later this week or early next; but remember, it's not a trial, and the merits of the case won't be discussed. A Justice of the Peace will assess whether there is a significant risk of you jumping bail. We will require the community's support, the community will have to vouch for you, and tell the court that you will not be a risk."

Rafiq looked at her, bewildered.

"Even if you're granted bail, which is not a certainty, there will be several restrictions placed upon you. It'll depend upon how the Crown argues the case and how the Justice of the Peace accepts our arguments."

When it was time for her to leave, she asked him: "If you were not involved, why did you save those emails?"

"To prove my innocence."

She shook her head, bemused at his naïveté.

—ɷ—

In his cell, Rafiq eventually drifted off to sleep. In his dream he was in a ravine; it looked like the one he would see from the window of the bus he took each morning. It was winter, and the foliage had withered away, the landscape a long barren stretch. A man was walking towards him from a distance. He was wearing a loose, open white shirt, and a lungi— a man's sarong—and a red-and-white chequered turban and sunglasses. He lugged a big suitcase. It had to be heavy because he shifted it from one hand to the other every few steps.

The man walked up to Rafiq. He smiled, put the suitcase down on its side and flicked it open. It contained a disassembled gun. He assembled it, and handed the gun to Rafiq. Rafiq wasn't sure he wanted to take it. From another direction, he heard a voice, faint at first but growing louder. It was Ammi's voice. She was shouting, "Don't, don't!" Rafiq stared at the man. He was Ghani Ahmed. He began to shout, but Rafiq couldn't hear a word. He only heard Ammi.

His mother was wearing a sari with a light blue floral print and dark blue border; Rafiq hadn't seen her in a sari since they had left India. She came rushing at them, and snatched the gun away from him. Ghani Ahmed said something to her that Rafiq couldn't hear. Ammi shouted, "No, my son isn't a murderer!" Ghani Ahmed smiled like wizard.

Rafiq tried to go up his mother, but he couldn't move, he was rooted to the spot. Suddenly, grass and foliage sprouted around his feet and began to grow; leaves and branches entwined him. He was turning into a tree. Ghani Ahmed grabbed the gun from his hands and fired it at Ammi, but she hid behind him. The spray of bullets had no impact on Rafiq or his mother because of the thick branches and leaves . . .

—ɷ—

Rafiq sat up on the bed, his heart beating fast. What a strange dream, he thought. Why was Ghani Ahmed wearing a lungi, and why was he trying to kill him and his mother?

He stretched out on the bed and calmed himself. He thought about the day's proceedings. Anita had told him that Ammi and Abba would come to meet him later that evening. Every time he had a moment to himself, his thoughts went back to his parents and he was filled with remorse. Ammi was soft, emotional, yet strong, and Abba was the guileless dreamer, unable to comprehend the world any more—so Rafiq had recently come to believe. He thought of Ghani Ahmed—the man who he thought had given him a new direction, a new life, a purpose and a mission in life, but he had been wrong, so thoroughly wrong. Was Abba right, after all? He realized he couldn't gainsay the experience of his parents. They had seen much of life, of people.

Until Anita asked him about it, Rafiq hadn't thought about his transition from Nagma Khala's overprotective care to Ghani Ahmed's radical mentoring, because it had happened gradually. There was no doubt that Ghani Ahmed's influence had made him more aware of Islam, how central it was to his existence—through his mother, primarily, and Nagma Khala, but also his sceptical father—and its place in Canadian society, where it wasn't accorded the consideration it deserved. He realized that for Ammi and Nagma Khala, Islam was a living faith, but for Ghani Ahmed it was about identity, it was about politics, about survival, about fighting back.

What had made him join Ghani Ahmed's mission? There were many reasons, most of them personal. He had seen how people from his neighbourhood, people like him, never really succeeded in Canada. All immigrants faced this problem, and everyone discussed it, but hadn't a clue about a solution. But it was different for Muslims. Not only were they not allowed to succeed, they were hated by mainstream Canada. Ammi and Abba were not alone, there were many like them who had to be satisfied with half-lives—unfulfilled lives—and it was especially difficult for Muslims to make the grade. His parents, steeped in their old-world ideals, were convinced that the system wasn't unjust, and they tried to adjust continuously. Every adjustment marginalized them, and they were sidelined ruthlessly.

He didn't know what one could do about an unjust system except fight it.

The 9/11 attacks happened a few days after his thirteenth birthday.

He remembered his father's distress. Abdul was furious with the terrorists and their Islamist ideology.

"These illiterate fanatics can't define Islam for us!" he said in a shrill voice, as they watched the Towers fall again and again on their TV. It seemed like the whole city around them had died.

But the men responsible for the attacks were not illiterate. Rafiq wanted to know more, to understand why educated and prosperous young men with a bright future were willing to sacrifice their lives. They had to believe deeply in what they were doing. Nagma Khala didn't have the answers, and his parents were not willing to talk about it. In the internet chat rooms, he found young Muslims finding links between Palestine, Afghanistan, Kashmir, Bosnia, and Chechnya.

After 9/11, school authorities across Toronto assured Muslim parents that the protection of their kids was a priority. There would be zero tolerance of bullying. Most Muslim students instinctively understood that non-Muslims viewed them with suspicion. They couldn't openly insult them, but they could make snide remarks and scrawl insults on locker doors and washroom walls.

One afternoon, when Rafiq was returning home from school with other kids from his building, a group of boys surrounded them. They were a mixed bunch: whites, blacks, Hispanics, South Asians even, but apparently not Muslims. One asked, "Who is Osama's son here?" He shoved the boy next to Rafiq. The boy stumbled.

Rafiq stepped forward. He said, "Please don't blame us."

It did no good. Someone pulled his shirt. Someone else pushed him in the chest. And then another pushed him harder and harder again, and he was surrounded by them. They pulled down his pants, his underwear, and pointed at his circumcised penis, they jeered.

"Osama's son!" they chanted.

The last thing he remembered before blacking out was a Nike sneaker with a piece of blue gum stuck to its sole, smashing into his face. He opened his eyes only when his companions sprinkled water on him. They took him home.

Rafiq feared more trouble if he told his parents about the incident, and he decided to keep quiet, but Ziram heard about it, and promptly told them. He expected them to be angry but, much to his surprise and subsequent dismay, they said nothing. The next day he was reluctant to go to school alone and Ammi and Abba accompanied him to meet the principal; she was sympathetic but stressed that the incident had not occurred in or around the school. Rafiq realized what it meant to be a Muslim in a country where Muslims were a minority. His parents had experienced it, and often spoken about it, but he hadn't been able to relate to it until that day. A few months before the boys who beat him up wouldn't have given him a second glance—but now they had become his mortal enemies.

His parents and Nagma Khala advised him to lie low to avoid trouble. Rafiq couldn't figure out why the elders were so defensive. He found it ironic that his parents, who claimed that they had left India so that their kids wouldn't have to face prejudice, kept quiet when he was brutalized in Canada. Afterwards, whenever his parents spoke about injustices against Muslims, he retorted, "You're hypocritical. You kept quiet when those goons kicked and punched me because I'm a Muslim."

For him and his family, everything changed after 9/11. Even the Bombay riots hadn't stayed in their minds the same way.

Seven

Ghani Ahmed used the MINA website to preach the right way of life for young Muslims growing up in an alien, Western culture. Sometime in 2004, Rafiq became drawn to the site, and he visited it frequently. He wrote to Ghani Ahmed after he listened to one of his webcasts, and he received an English translation of the Quran in the mail, in which Ghani Ahmed had inscribed, "This will show you the right path." Soon they were exchanging emails. Rafiq started receiving email messages everyday, which began with a brief passage from the Quran, followed by detailed news about the persecution of Muslims around the world.

Ghani Ahmed's thesis was that after 9/11 the world order had turned against Muslims. The United States invaded Iraq, causing the deaths of more than a hundred thousand Muslims, and destroyed Baghdad. In 2002, less than a year after 9/11, thousands of Muslims were killed in Gujarat, India. Canada joined NATO forces in Afghanistan and became an accomplice in the ongoing massacre of Muslims. Ghani Ahmed argued that the Jews had faced persecution and genocide because they never rose against the Nazis; had they united and retaliated they wouldn't have suffered. His solution was simple—unity and retaliation. Rafiq was completely taken in, convinced that Ghani Ahmed was right. The email exchanges continued apace, Ghani Ahmed even sending him video clips of Osama bin Laden's messages to jihadists worldwide.

Rafiq once asked Ghani Ahmed in an email about his background, where he hailed from.

"I'm Allah's servant and that is all that matters," was the cryptic answer.

The offensive cartoons of Prophet Mohammed in Denmark and their swift spread across Europe and Canada underscored Ghani Ahmed's arguments that the Western world despised Islam, even when it used the language of peace and reason. In 2006, the cartoons were published in Canada. It was at this time that Ghani Ahmed asked Rafiq to meet him.

Rafiq took a bus to a boxy restaurant in a strip mall in Meadowvale, Mississauga. The place was empty except for a Punjabi family of six. Two sides of the restaurant had windows, and the other two had walls draped in a dark-brown velvety material. A large painting on the wall above the kitchen door depicted a family inside a home in rural Punjab—a mother sitting on the floor and cooking, a father smoking a hookah, and three kids of varying ages frolicking in the foreground. Rafiq sat at a table facing the door. Ghani Ahmed hadn't arrived yet.

Eventually a man strode in through the door and walked over purposefully to Rafiq's table. He was stocky but not fat, and wore a tweed jacket and blue jeans; he was nearly bald with a greying beard. He didn't remove his gold-rimmed Ray Ban aviators but smiled briefly, before embracing Rafiq three times in the traditional Islamic greeting. There was a whiff of perfume on him.

"I see you have grown a beard as I advised," Ghani Ahmed said, studying Rafiq's face. "Sit, sit. Did you have something to eat?" He spoke in the manner of wealthy South Asians—Abba called it the accent of the "convent-educated."

"No, I was waiting for you."

"We must have lunch first, and then talk."

He ordered a lamb rogan josh, four kulchas, two dal makhanis, and jeera rice. For starters, he asked for hara-bhara kababs, accompanied by two glasses of iced tea. Ghani Ahmed seemed to know the people here, and Rafiq thought he must eat there often. He relaxed.

Before they started to eat, Ghani Ahmed went to the men's room to wash his hands. When he returned, he asked Rafiq to change places, so he could watch the entrance.

"I want your support," he said later, leaning forward and speaking in an earnest and sincere-sounding tone.

"You have my support, sir. What should I do?"

"You wrote to me that you had raised funds for victims of the

Kashmir earthquake last year."

Rafiq nodded.

"I want you to get involved with our work. We are organizing a camp in Kathmandu in Nepal for young Muslims from North America and Europe. They will get together and share their experiences of living in an alien culture which doesn't respect Islam."

"I don't have the money to go there," Rafiq said hesitatingly.

"We'll pay, you don't have to worry about a thing."

Rafiq nodded uncertainly. He couldn't hide his disappointment. He was expecting more than just a trip to the subcontinent. Ghani Ahmed cupped his mouth as he dug a toothpick in and eyed him keenly.

"After you return, we will wake up the Canadians."

Ghani Ahmed leaned forward and spoke in a lowered voice, "I have a plan for that. But we'll discuss it later, after you return from Kathmandu."

Rafiq nodded.

Ghani Ahmed then began to talk about the serial bombing in Bombay that had ripped through the suburban train network earlier that year, killing 150 commuters and injuring hundreds more. He spoke passionately and with admiration about the 2005 London bombings and the 2004 Madrid attack, how meticulously they had been planned and executed.

"That is the only language they understand," Ghani Ahmed said. "We must also eventually kick Canada in the balls."

Rafiq looked at him searchingly, unsure what to say or do.

Before leaving, Ghani Ahmed gave Rafiq a copy of his book, *My Dreams*.

The trip to Kathmandu had been an utter waste of time, as was the visit to Ahmedabad in India. Then in early 2007 he received the first of a series of emails from Ghani Ahmed about the bombing plot in Toronto. Two of these emails had been discovered by Ziram and Abba, which was why he was now here, in prison.

"It's time to wake up the Canadians," Ghani Ahmed said in his email. "We bomb Toronto: our target is Canada."

"That will cause a bloodbath," Rafiq remembered thinking, as he read through that email. The man continued to talk casually about ways to kill hundreds of people. He wanted Rafiq to start working on mapping potential targets across Toronto. Rafiq didn't want to be part of the plan, but Ghani Ahmed assumed Rafiq's total commitment, and Rafiq didn't know how to speak his mind.

He tried to wriggle out of the assignment by arguing that the mapping was unnecessary, since Google had mapped out all of North America. Ghani Ahmed wrote back saying he wanted more details—for example, the number of chairs in the waiting lounge at Finch subway station, and the number of garbage bins in the food court at Square One Mall. From these maps and details he would select seven sites. Reluctantly, Rafiq travelled around the Greater Toronto Area, scouting for possible targets.

Rafiq was determined to find a way out of this involvement. That moment came when he was reconnoitring the Square One Mall in Mississauga. In the food court, he ordered kebabs from a place that proudly advertised halal food. A young mother, wearing a hijab and accompanied by a little boy and girl, sat down at the next table. The enormity of Ghani Ahmed's plan hit him as he looked around him. There were hundreds of families in the mall that Sunday afternoon, and most of them weren't even white. They were like him, his family.

That evening when he emailed the Google maps of seven sites to Ghani Ahmed, he also wrote saying that he agreed with his mentor's political and religious views, but he wasn't going to do anything that would lead to a bloodbath, because he was convinced that revenge against a callous system shouldn't involve massacre of innocent people. It was inhuman and against the tenets of Islam. Ghani Ahmed didn't respond.

Disturbed that he had collaborated on a blueprint for mass murder he tried to talk to his father. It was impossible to confess anything to Abba, because well before he could even get close to the subject, his dad, in his usual manner, would begin a lecture.

"Muslims have every reason to be angry but the solution is dialogue, not terrorism."

"Nobody was willing to talk to you when you lost everything in India," Rafiq once countered, exasperated at Abba's meaningless idealism.

"You have grown up, haven't you?"

"Do you think coming here solved your problems?"

"We thought Canada would be different."

"And it isn't, right?"

"Well . . ."

"Precisely. That's what I mean."

His dad didn't ask what he meant, and Rafiq lost the will to tell him about Ghani Ahmed. He had only confused himself. By arguing against Abba he had begun to sound like Ghani Ahmed.

—⁓—

In his cell Rafiq waited impatiently for his parents. Having unburdened himself to Anita, he was now keen to confess everything to Abba and Ammi and convince them that he wasn't the terrorist the police accused him to be, or they imagined him to be. Abdul and Ruksana drove to Maplehurst late in the afternoon. The place smelled of air freshener. As trade union activists in Bombay, both Abdul and Ruksana had seen the inside of a prison many times. This was their first visit to a prison in Canada. Ruksana couldn't help but compare the difference between the rundown lockups in India with this one, which looked better than the apartment building that had been their home for more than a decade.

A security officer directed them to an enclosed visitors' lounge behind the main door, where they completed the formalities for meeting their son. Another officer then led them to a large room that resembled a cafeteria or an assembly hall in a school. There were several tables and chairs here. Absence of natural light and air gave the room a musty smell and moist feel; their footsteps on the wooden floor echoed loudly.

They were asked to sit at a table. Both looked around the room, and nervously exchanged glances. The few visitors and inmates had all chosen to sit at tables well away from each other to be able to talk in privacy. As they sat waiting, another officer led Rafiq in from another door. The parents expected the officers to leave the room, but they didn't, merely stood at some distance from the table. Rafiq looked tired and disoriented, his hair was tousled and his eyes were swollen. His beard had grown and turned scraggly. His prison uniform was too big for him. Ruksana found it hard to reconcile the two sides to her son. Which one was the real Rafiq: the seemingly helpless young lad sitting across from them, or the tough young man who had glared in silent defiance at them when he was arrested? She suppressed a sob.

"You look tired," Abdul said.

Rafiq looked at his parents and began to weep. "I haven't slept," he said.

"Where do they keep you? Does the place have a bed?"

"In a small cell, alone."

"Yes, Anita told us that the isolation is supposed to be for your own protection. Did you eat anything?"

"I'm sorry I've caused so many problems," he said, looking at his Ammi.

She fought back tears. "Did you meet the lawyer?"

"Yes. I answered all her questions."

"What did she ask?"

"About Ahmed Saab and . . . "

"Beta, that man destroyed your life . . . our lives . . . and you still call him 'Saab'?"

Ruksana raised her hand to stop Rafiq from explaining, and said, "Your Abba and I have worked long and hard, but I realize we have failed to make you a good human being."

Rafiq was quiet. Abdul stared at Ruksana, concerned that she was speaking so harshly.

"Rafiq, we shouldn't have called Ravindar before talking to you."

"Abba, I wanted to tell you everything for a long time. I didn't want to hide anything. I didn't tell you because I wasn't sure."

"Did Anita say anything specific?"

"She thinks I may not have all the answers. I told her I believe

Ahmed Saab—Ghani Ahmed—had dropped me from his group."

"But we got a call from Ghani Ahmed's friends yesterday, asking us if we need any help . . . " Abdul's voice was flat, his gaze fixed on Rafiq.

"I don't know anything about that."

Abdul felt his son was hiding more than he was telling.

"Have they interrogated you?"

"No, but Anita told me they'll do so soon."

"Any problems?"

"Not yet."

"Don't talk without consulting Anita first. Tell them you won't talk without a lawyer," Abdul said, and then asked: "Beta why did you do all this?"

"You're angry because I've gone against your thinking. I'm sorry about that, but believe me, I wasn't involved in the plot, except initially. I didn't know better. I've already told that to Anita."

Abdul looked at him resignedly. "I wish I could believe you. Ziram found that book written by Ghani Ahmed in your room. She says it is garbage. I also read some pages; I agree with her. I may not be as religious as you, but I know the difference between religion and rubbish."

Rafiq's expression, in return, was spiteful. "Ammi, I'm sorry," he repeated.

"Let us pray to Allah that you are safe. We can't do much, but you shouldn't lose hope. Pray five times, and read from the Quran so that you have peace of mind."

"Did you call Hameed Surti?"

"No, we didn't, but we will," Ruksana lied. Actually, Hameed Surti, the owner of Wanderlust, Rafiq's employer, had called a day after Rafiq's arrest to ask why he hadn't shown up, and Ziram had to tell him about the arrest. Hameed had politely offered to help the family but they were too embarrassed even to talk to him.

It was time to leave. Rafiq was taken away.

—◊◊◊—

The officer who had brought them to the room now led Abdul and

Ruksana out, and took them into an office in the main visitors' enclosure.

"Please wait here, one of our officers wants to talk to you," the man said and left the room. The room was empty. It had no windows. There was a large, dark brown sofa and two chairs, a large wooden table. Three of the four walls had similar-looking framed photographs of trees, mountains, and the sun. The fourth wall had the door.

Abdul and Ruksana looked at each other as they sat on the sofa. They waited nervously for some time, and then Abdul got up impatiently and tried to open the door.

"The knob won't turn, the door is locked," he said, turning to Ruksana.

"Why don't we wait, someone will surely come," Ruksana replied.

"But how can they just lock us in here?" Abdul said, and again tried to turn the knob.

"Let me try," she said, coming over. She tried, without success. "It is locked from outside."

Abdul banged the door hard. "Open the door!" he shouted, but there was no response. He glanced at his watch. "It is not closing time yet." He banged harder.

"The guard must have been delayed. He will open the door when he returns," Ruksana said, "we'll have to just wait for some time."

"You sit. I will wait here," Abdul said, and banged on the door again. He paced the room, while Ruksana shuffled uncomfortably on the sofa. After about five minutes he banged on the door again but to no avail.

"Call Anita," Ruksana said.

"They took away the cellphone when we came in here, remember?" She asked Abdul to sit down, but he wouldn't.

"Take it easy Saabji," Ruksana said. She was nervous that he would lose control. She began to recite the Surah Yasin Sharif from the Quran. To her the Surah encapsulated the true essence of the Quran—Allah's omniscience and one's accountability for one's deeds—and she recited it whenever she needed divine support. It gave her the strength to face difficulties.

The door remained locked. Abdul banged again and shouted at the top of his voice. The situation was agonizing, frightening.

Finally someone, a different officer, opened the door. Abdul wanted to shower him with abuses, but Ruksana held his hand to restrain him.

"We thought you had left," the officer said.

"No, we were told that someone wanted to talk to us and we were brought to this room," Abdul said. He was short of breath.

"Thank you for opening the door," Ruksana said politely.

"Who wanted to talk to us, and about what?" Abdul asked.

"I'm Shawn. I look after your son here. I wanted to know more about your son and his friend."

"But we don't know anything," Abdul said.

"Your son lived with you, how can you claim you don't know anything? You can trust me. If there's anything that you want to share with me, do so and I promise you it'll remain between us."

"We are telling you the truth. Would we have informed the police about the emails if we wanted to hide anything?" Ruksana asked gently.

Shawn looked at her and nodded. He then led them out of the room and to the main door.

Abdul called Anita as soon as they were outside and told her what had happened. "Should we complain to the superintendent?"

"Let me think about it. You two take it easy, go home and rest."

II

The Trade Union Leader

Eight

Back home, Ruksana's thoughts drifted to Dhinmant. He had been her saviour, mentor, and friend, with whom she had shared a relationship that neither of them felt the need to define. He had turned her from a gauche, small-town girl into a poised and confident woman. Since Rafiq's arrest, she had repeatedly asked herself, "What would Dhinmant have done?" He wouldn't have called the police before talking to Rafiq. That was the crucial difference between Dhinmant and Abdul. Her husband's responses were always based on principles, whereas Dhinmant generally thought through the consequences before he acted.

Dhinmant had been special to Abdul, too. But in Canada, Abdul's respect for him had turned into resentment. Over the years, especially in Canada, Ruksana had learned the hard lesson of not talking about Dhinmant. She had stopped trying to explain their relationship to her husband, not because there was anything to hide, but because she knew that her husband had come to believe that she and Dhinmant had been, if not lovers, at least too close. She herself thought this belief comforted him, made him feel more like a martyr at a time when his life was not particularly happy. It was simpler for Ruksana to let Abdul feel the way he did.

Abdul fell into a dour silence whenever Ruksana brought up Teli Gali, the oil-sellers' alley, their old suburban neighbourhood in Bombay. She tried to talk to him about their old neighbours, people who had been their friends, but Abdul refused to warm up to the memories. He wanted to forget Teli Gali, forget that he had lived there all his life, forget that it was there that he had first met Dhinmant and Ruksana— and because he couldn't quite forget, he would snap at her, "Forget what happened there, live your life in the present."

For Ruksana, it was impossible to forget Dhinmant. He had sheltered and protected her when she was lost and alone. He occupied a large space in her heart. But had she ever loved him? Ruksana denied this vehemently to Abdul, and to herself, perhaps a touch too vehemently. She didn't want to call it love; adoration perhaps, but not love. Love was only among equals; but one adored someone superior.

Ruksana found it hard to come to terms with Abdul's change of heart towards Dhinmant's memory. Who was the real Abdul—the one in India who had vowed to fight to bring to justice Dhinmant's murderers? Or the one in Canada, whose face clouded every time she brought up Dhinmant? She often wondered at the irony: she had had to dissuade Abdul from dragging the local police and the state to court to prove their complicity in Dhinmant's murder, and the massacre of hundreds of people. Now the mere mention of Dhinmant got his blood on the boil.

In December 1992, Hindu fundamentalists demolished a mosque in the temple town of Ayodhya, the birthplace of the Hindu God Ram, claiming that it had been built over a temple that was Ram's birthplace. The result across India, including Bombay, was a month of the most vicious, horrific and prolonged religious violence.

One evening in January 1993, while Abdul and Dhinmant sat in the union office in Teli Gali discussing the unprecedented butchery in their city, they heard the roar of a mob approaching. Dhinmant told Abdul to take his car, drive to the police station, and bring his friend, Inspector Sandeep Waghmare. As a precaution, however, Abdul took Ruksana and the two kids along with him. Leaving them at the police station, he then returned to Teli Gali with the inspector.

Ruksana and the kids sat on one of the three wooden benches in the visitors' room in the station. Large black-and-white photographs of Mahatma Gandhi, Jawaharlal Nehru, and Indira Gandhi hung on the walls, which were painted beige at the top and dark brown at the bottom (the darker colour apparently to hide the paan-spit stains). A fan whirled dangerously overhead, sounding like a tornado but generating little breeze. A naked bulb occasionally flickered but barely lit the room.

It was close to midnight, but the police station was bustling. People came and went, the wireless radio crackled every few minutes with news about a new outbreak of violence in the city. Ruksana kept busy swatting mosquitoes that were hovering over her kids, who were asleep on the bench, their heads resting on her thighs. She had wrapped her dupatta around seven-year-old Ziram, and pages from a newspaper around five-year-old Rafiq. It gave her something to do, to keep her sanity in a world going mad all around her. But not for long.

Ruksana would always remember her stifled scream—her palms clasped to her mouth—when Abdul phoned from Cooper Hospital and told her that their home had burned down. He had sounded surprisingly calm. He told her that the mob had ransacked Teli Gali and beaten up Dhinmant. Neighbours had rushed him to the hospital. Abdul himself was safe and Inspector Waghmare was with him. She had wanted to go to the hospital, but Abdul ordered her to wait for him. He would come to fetch her at daybreak: it was too risky for either of them to be out.

Just before dawn Abdul returned with Inspector Waghmare. Ruksana was praying in a corner of the visitors' room. That night, too, she hadn't asked anything of Allah. The ride from the police station to the hospital was eerie; the road was littered with charred vehicles still smouldering. When they reached Cooper Hospital, Ruksana saw workers from Dhinmant's union waving a banner, shouting, "Dhinmant Desai Amar Rahe!" at the main gate. "Long live Dhinmant Desai." She was frightened. When they reached the intensive care unit, a nurse told Abdul, "Your leader is dead."

—⁓—

Ruksana was determined not to let Dhinmant's murder defeat her. While Abdul vowed revenge and made elaborate plans to go to court, Ruksana studied other options. She had no illusions about getting justice in a society where the law worked for those who were rich and well-connected, and they were neither. But more than anything else, she was also convinced that Muslims couldn't get justice in India at a time when the country was surging with Hindu nationalism.

She diverted Abdul's energies. She made him sell his ancestral land in Gorakhpur in Uttar Pradesh, and the plot of land in Teli Gali on which their home and office had stood. They hired an immigration agency, which advised them that they could reach Canada sooner on a tourist visa. Once there, they could apply for refugee status as persecuted members of a minority religion.

A year later—in 1995—they landed in Toronto. The agency helped them secure refugee status, and got them permanent-resident cards. They didn't face procedural problems, because everything that had happened to them had been well documented in the international media. Soon after they arrived, they were confronted with their poverty. They realized that perpetual penury was to be their fate in Canada, but it still didn't shake their conviction that the new land was good for their kids. They hadn't wanted them to grow up in a society that looked upon Muslims with suspicion and constantly questioned their loyalty.

—�w—

Ruksana was certain that everything would work out fine eventually— that had been her experience. She had once before been forced to flee from one life into another. That traumatic and tragic change had also brought with it unprecedented happiness. She met Abdul, fell in love with him, and married him.

—�w—

She had lived with her parents in Islampura, a Muslim neighbourhood in Sarhupur, a town in Uttar Pradesh in Northern India. Her father, Ibrahim, was a clerk in the local government office, and her mother, Mahejabeen, worked at home and tended the family's small vegetable garden in the backyard. An only child, Ruksana was protected and sheltered. But that had helped her become fiercely independent.

She fled Sarhupur when mobs ransacked the town after upper-caste Thakur farmers massacred the lower-caste Jatava peasants, who were celebrating the four-day festival of the Goddess, called Durga Puja.

Affronted by this innocent act of piety, the Thakurs proclaimed that Mother Durga had been defiled by the lower caste. Thakur gangs left a trail of death and destruction, and then they turned their ire against the Muslims, who had provided the decorations for the festival.

When a mob of upper-caste goons reached their home, Ruksana's mother forced her to jump into the well in their backyard. Ruksana stayed inside, keeping afloat by holding onto a rope and clutching at the moss-covered brick walls. After what seemed a lifetime, she cautiously climbed out. Wrapping her arms around her breasts, dripping from head to toe, her salwaar khameez clinging to her body, she tiptoed into the kitchen. There, her mother sat on the floor beside her father. Blood flowed from his neck. Her mother murmured, "Maar dala—they killed him," over and over, unable to stop. She was too numb to cry.

Once Ruksana confirmed that her father was dead, she knew that she and her mother had to escape the mobs still roaming the narrow streets. She tugged at her mother, whispering, "Chalo Ma, we must flee." Her mother obeyed her like a child, and Ruksana pulled her along the path in the paddy field behind their home. Her mother tried to keep pace with her but collapsed in exhaustion.

A tractor with wagon came their way from the town. When it passed them, she saw that the wagon was filled with bodies. The tractor coughed to a halt not far from where they were hiding, and the aged driver alighted to smoke a beedie. Ruksana decided to take a chance. She walked hesitatingly to the tractor, dragging her mother along. The driver examined her from head to toe and said, "Get in and lie with the bodies. There may be a few still alive. You are on your own if someone checks."

Ruksana pushed her mother into the wagon. Clambering over bodies, she found a place to sit. The old driver restarted his journey, and after they had gone some distance and reached a railway crossing, she called out to him to stop. She pulled at her mother's hand to help her get up. But her mother was dead. Ruksana didn't know what to do.

The driver came around and told her, "She is dead. You can't do anything about it. Go away, save yourself."

Tears streaming down her face, she told the driver, "Mahejabeen . . . Muslim . . . bury her." She had no idea what would happen to her father's body.

The driver gave her a two-rupee note and drove away.

Ruksana had planned to take her mother to her uncle's place near Moradabad, but now she wasn't sure what to do. She didn't want to return to Sarhupur. After a long trudge along the railway tracks under a sweltering sun, she reached a station where a train was at the platform. Boarding it without a ticket, she reached Agra a little after midnight. Hungry, exhausted, she got off and sat on a bench not knowing what to do or where to go.

A train screeched to a halt on the opposite platform, and she was surprised to see the sleepy station come alive with vendors. She asked a tea-seller boy where the train was headed. "Bambai. It is the Amritsar-Dadar Express," he replied contemptuously, irritated that this straggly girl was wasting his time. She climbed aboard.

Ruksana made a place for herself on the floor near the door of the unreserved coach. The acrid stench from the nearby toilet made her clutch her nose. The coach was crammed with passengers, the unlucky taking floor space, the lucky ones the wooden benches, all fitfully trying to sleep. The lights in the coach flickered, the fans weren't working, and the coach was like the hot interior of a tandoor oven, even though the windows were open. Ruksana was uncomfortable, her hair was dishevelled and she felt dirty in her soiled salwaar khameez. She had no idea what she was going to do in Bombay. She wanted to pray but there was no place.

An upper-class woman on a bench, a man beside her, was looking at her intently. They didn't belong in the unreserved coach. The woman waved a cardboard fan at her sweating face. She was slender and dark-skinned like Ruksana, and wore a plain grey cotton sari; a thick pair of brown glasses was prominent on her face, making her eyes and nose look small.

The solidly built man beside her was almost bald, his pate shining with sweat. He often raised his glasses to wipe the sweat out of his eyes.

He had a big, round face and an oversized nose. His white cotton shirt was crumpled, with large wet patches in the underarms. He had rolled up his black trousers up to his ankles. He pulled out a file from a bulging cloth bag at his feet and began to read. The woman kept looking at her but Ruksana wasn't sure whether she should return her gaze. Finally the woman whispered something to her companion; he stopped reading and looked towards Ruksana. After a moment's hesitation, he came over.

"My name is Dhinmant Desai. I can help you." Despite Ruksana's suspicion and fear, the man's sympathy reduced her to tears.

Nonplussed by Ruksana's tears, the man looked back to the woman, who came over. "I told him to talk to you. I'm Kinnari," she said in a gentle voice.

"Where are you going?" the man asked.

"Get up, come and sit with us." The woman put her hand on Ruksana's shoulder.

Ruksana couldn't stop crying. Disturbed from their sleep, the other passengers sat up, watching them. Dhinmant told them—in an authoritative voice that people from big cities in India unconsciously, and automatically use when talking to those from India's villages— that everything was all right. Kinnari asked a passenger sitting by the window to shift a little. The man reluctantly made room. Kinnari offered Ruksana water from her pink plastic water bag, and Dhinmant gave her a packet of deep fried potato bhujiyas. She hadn't eaten for several hours and finished the packet quickly.

"I'm Dhinmant and she is my wife Kinnari. What is your name? Where are you going?"

"Ruksana."

"Where are you going?"

She didn't answer.

"Where have you come from?" He sounded a bit impatient.

"Sarhupur."

"There are riots in that area. Are you all right? Are you alone?" Kinnari asked, her voice rising with her concern.

Ruksana cried again.

"Leave her alone for a while," Dhinmant said, sitting back.

Kinnari disregarded him. "This train is going to Bombay. Do you know anyone there?"

They seemed kind and decent, and she would eventually have to trust someone. Almost inaudibly, Ruksana said, "Why should I tell you? I don't know who you are."

Kinnari smiled and patted her shoulder reassuringly.

"We are from a trade union in Bombay. Do you know what a trade union is?" she asked.

She pulled out a fresh set of salwaar khameez from her bag. "Come with me to the toilet and change into these clothes. They aren't your size but you need clean clothes." Ruksana was reluctant.

"Trust me. You are like my sister," Kinnari said.

Clutching the clothes and holding her nose, Ruksana entered the stinking toilet of the coach. It was hard for her to keep her balance with the rocking and rattling of the train. She tried to wash her face, but the tap was dry; she opened the door, and asked Kinnari if she had water. Kinnari got her plastic water bottle. Ruksana looked down at the clean clothes, they smelled good. She would think about what to do when she got to Bombay. Maybe she could go to Govandi. She had heard her mother talk about her cousin who lived in Govandi, a suburb of Bombay.

Kinnari told her that they lived and worked in Andheri, another suburb of Bombay. Dhinmant led the Bombay Textile Workers Union, and Kinnari worked with quarry workers in Powai. Ruksana looked at her, wide-eyed. Kinnari was vivacious and charming and had a natural, friendly manner. Dhinmant was again busy reading his papers.

Ruksana couldn't sleep and observed the stars from her window as the train tore through the darkness; she was leaving behind her past and rushing into an uncertain future.

"Not able to sleep?" Kinnari asked.

Ruksana nodded. She pulled up her legs on the seat, and put her arms around her knees. She was tired. Kinnari patted her knees and said, "You will feel better if you talk and we may be able to help you."

Haltingly Ruksana told them about the religious violence she had witnessed. She couldn't stop weeping.

"Where are your parents?" Kinnari asked.

"Dead."

"Everything will be all right," Kinnari whispered, and wiped away her tears. "You are very brave." She pulled Ruksana nearer to her and gently patted her head. "You can come with us. You can stay at the union office."

Ruksana smiled faintly. She fell asleep soon after, and the couple woke her as the train reached Bombay. It was still dark outside. She gagged at the stench that flowed in through the window, and hastily pulled her dupatta over her nose.

"Welcome to Bombay," Dhinmant said, laughing heartily. "You are lucky it isn't yet daylight. In the morning you can see grown men defecating along the railway tracks."

Ruksana looked at him disbelievingly, and Kinnari chided him, "There is nothing to laugh about poverty." She told Ruksana, "These people live in slums, they don't have a proper home, and so they have to do their morning business on the tracks. It is particularly difficult for women. They have to do it in darkness at night."

She looked out again. The suburban railway stations passed by and she saw that even at this early hour people were thronging the stations. She was now in Bombay, a city she had seen in the movies. One city with three names: Bombay, Bambai and Mumbai. She was excited but scared, too.

In the pre-dawn twilight, Dadar station didn't look any different from Agra except for the massive crowds. She had never seen so many people, not even at the annual mela in Sarhupur, and she wondered if there were so many people now, what would the station be like in daylight. Ruksana followed the couple through the crowd, as a porter carried their luggage in front. She was awestruck by the sights and the sounds. So many vehicles and so many lights.

She caught up with Kinnari and tightly gripped her arm. They got into a taxi and in half-an-hour reached Teli Gali. The taxi stopped in front of a decrepit one-storey house within a compound, next to a ramshackle old shed. A signboard in nagari script over the shed said Bombay Textile Workers Union. The signboard was new and lit by a bulb. Just then she heard the muezzin's call to prayer. Ruksana covered her head with her dupatta. The mosque had to be close by because the azaan was loud.

"We work here," Dhinmant said. "It is our office. We live further down the lane in a bungalow."

"You can come with us," Kinnari said. "Or you can stay here. There is an empty room."

"Who else is there?" Ruksana asked. The office was no better than the cattle shed in her neighbour's backyard in Sarhupur.

"Nobody. Abdul owns the place, but he lives in that house with his father Shamsuddin," Dhinmant said, pointing to another building in the compound.

"I will stay here," Ruksana said. Even though the office seemed run-down, she was already feeling better, hearing Muslim names, and of the proximity of the office to a masjid. She gingerly followed Dhinmant inside.

"Abdul should be here later. If you need anything, just knock on his door. You can trust him. We will tell him that you are here," Kinnari said.

After they left, Ruksana locked the door. She went to the washroom. It was smelly, and she made a mental note to clean it. The orange plastic bucket was full and she was glad to have a bath. Then she cleansed herself, and offered the namaaz in Dhinmant's office. Allah would give her the strength to start her new life.

The office had two rooms. The main room, Dhinmant's workplace, had beat-up furniture. What caught her attention was the telephone. She had seen one at the post office in Sarhupur. She picked up the receiver, and put it to her ear. It buzzed. She rotated a few digits, said "Hello" and then quickly put it down. Ruksana looked out the window. Although still early in the morning, the traffic outside on the intersection was gradually thickening. She was fascinated by the different types of vehicles, and clapped her hands at the sight of a red double-decker bus.

With daylight, the traffic bestirred itself into a muted roar, a sleeping monster coming alive. She heard a knock on the door.

"Who is it?"

"Abdul," the voice said.

When she opened the door she saw a young man with a thermos flask in one hand and a cup in another. He was smiling at her.

"You came with Dhinmant?"

Suddenly self-conscious, she covered her head with her dupatta.

"Here, have some chai."

"I haven't brushed my teeth yet. I will go and do that."

"There is toothpaste in the bathroom. I will get a toothbrush for you today. For now, use your finger."

She went to the bathroom. Abdul seemed about the same age as she, and about the same height. He had small eyes, and a large nose that made everything else on his face look small. He had a large forehead, and long ears, but what she found most striking about him was his fair complexion.

"I forgot to ask your name," he said as he waited for her to come out of the washroom.

"Ruksana Syed."

"Abdul Latif."

"I guessed," Ruksana said and smiled.

Nine

Abdul was sitting on his red armchair in the bedroom, a woollen shawl over his legs and a small pillow behind his back. Ruksana was sleeping restlessly. Occasionally he would turn to throw a look of concern at her, and then he would turn back towards the emptiness outside, which gave him so much comfort. He sensed the wind from the swaying of the branches, the moonlight giving them gnarled bony shadows. When it wasn't too cold—and sometimes even when it was—he would go downstairs and step out briefly to listen to the rustle of the leaves, and feel the wind on his face. He loved to walk barefoot on the grass in the summer.

Abdul liked the dry Canadian wind. It was different from the moist and sticky sea breeze of Bombay. In the not-quite-warm spring, the all-too-brief summer, and the ominously chilly fall, he often sat on the front lawn, taking in the morning sun. He loved the ripe shade of magenta on the leaves in early spring, and the starkly bare branches of late fall. Canada offered so much more of nature, yet for many years he had lived far above the ground in an apartment, condemned to merely see, not actually experience and live surrounded by nature.

When they moved into their townhouse, he was for the first time in his life so close to nature—a patch of green in front, and trees lining the street. He marvelled at the vastness of the sky in Mississauga. It took him back to his childhood in Gorakhpur, where the sky was as expansive and richly hued. But there, birds chirped all through the day. Here, birds were heard only in spring and summer.

Abdul was feeling lost, defeated. Rafiq's ambiguity enraged him. He couldn't get over his son's involvement with Ghani Ahmed. He was shocked that his son couldn't see the difference between protesting against an unjust system and planting bombs in public places. Rafiq claimed he was against the murder of innocents, and yet called a rank terrorist like Ghani Ahmed "Saab" out of respect. Had he known about this earlier, Abdul would have drilled some common sense into his son, but now it was too late. Then he wondered whether he would actually have spoken to Rafiq, had he known. He probably wouldn't have.

Canada had changed him—it had silenced him. He always felt exhausted, and he had felt this way for a long time. In Canada he had lost his self-confidence. In India he was always in control. Dhinmant had needed him to start his trade union. Ruksana had needed him to restart her life. Here he needed his family even to perform simple tasks. Along with his confidence, he had also lost his former easy ways. He couldn't recall the last time he had laughed. He had become aware of this internal transformation in him, and he had tried to resist it. But it was an uneven fight, against himself and his circumstances; he couldn't win.

Canada had defeated him. At first he had thought that it was because of the language. Everyone said it was a major hurdle, but he had seen people who knew absolutely no English thrive. Kartar, who spoke with a more pronounced accent than Abdul did, was a great example. When he was a newcomer, Abdul had joined ESL classes to improve his English and learned other skills to equip himself to survive, but he couldn't learn the most basic skill required in Canada—the art of self-promotion, and a complete conviction in one's abilities, even if there were none.

Ruksana's attitude had changed, too. After a few years of working hard at it, she had abandoned all attempts to adjust and mingle, and instead sought solace in her Islamic faith. It was only slightly different for Abdul. He was impatient with religion, and the necessity of earning a living forced him to interact with people. Neither of them felt at home in Canada, and India only reminded them of their loss.

Abdul tried hard not to lose sight of the fact that their main reason to leave India had been to give their kids better choices. He had joined Sloan Auto, doing odd jobs initially and gradually rising to do office work. Later he had applied for several jobs that required administrative skills, but he didn't have either a formal qualification or any demonstrable experience. He had joined many networking groups and immigrants' forums but they didn't help. He was stuck at Sloan Auto, and had been there till his recent layoff.

He wouldn't have a proper career in Canada, but he was consoled by the thought that Ziram and Rafiq would get ahead in life. He had never tried to influence their thinking or opinions in any way, preferring to let them find their own paths. He was happy that Ziram was an independent woman. He had also been confident that despite Rafiq's difficulties in adjusting to his new environment, he would eventually come around and settle down. When Rafiq started working at Wanderlust, Abdul felt vindicated. But now it had all fallen apart. He just couldn't come to terms with Rafiq's betrayal.

In his heart, Abdul blamed both Ghani Ahmed and Canadian society equally. Ghani Ahmed misguided young, impressionable minds. Canada effortlessly made its Muslim population feel unwanted in different ways. He just couldn't fathom why everyone—from political parties to law courts—made such a big deal out of some Muslim women's preference of covering their heads with a piece of cloth. He found this paradoxical because he was convinced that Canada was liberal, progressive, and tolerant. Rafiq, of course, argued that the much-touted notion of freedom and democracy in Western societies was reserved for white people.

—⁂—

These days, Abdul often recalled his father's words. Whenever Abdul was disappointed, Shamsuddin would put a hand on his shoulder and say, "Manzil sab ko nasib nahin hoti—Not everyone has the good fortune to reach their destination." When they moved to their townhouse—their own Manzil—both he and Ruksana had believed that they were finally reaching their destination. He had often wondered how his father had coped with his own disappointments. Like many others, Shamsuddin had come to Bombay with the dream of becoming a movie star but eventually accepted that he could never be more than a film extra. Abdul admired his father's memory, because he had never abandoned his dreams even as he struggled to make his children's lives better than his life had been.

Shamsuddin had left his wife Ameena and his kids, three-year-old Abdul and his baby sister Afraa, behind in Gorakhpur to come to Bombay to become rich and famous. He became neither. He rented a house in Teli Gali, a walking distance from all the major movie studios. A few years later, still unsuccessful, he called his family to Teli Gali, where not long afterwards Ameena died of tuberculosis. Shamsuddin was still in his early thirties. He resisted family pressure to remarry, and stayed single, caring for two growing kids, and abandoned his dream of becoming a film star to become an agent for film extras.

Teli Gali is no longer known by its old name. The city renamed it after Dhinmant, calling it the Dhinmant Desai Marg. When Abdul read about the name change in Canada, he laughed bitterly.

"Deify those whose ideas you hate, it makes them irrelevant," he said to Ruksana.

When Abdul failed for the second time in his final year at school, his father decided not to waste time or money sending him to college or allowing him to "turn into a loafer." Using his network of friends, he got him a taxi license and bought a new Premier Padmini taxi. At seventeen, Abdul became an earning member of their small family, abandoning his own dream of commuting in the suburban train to an office in south Bombay: fulfilling that required a college education, but Shamsuddin insisted that he earn first and then bankroll his dream if he still desired it.

One day Abdul happened to shuttle an intriguing passenger called Raju from Metro Cinema to Andheri. Raju asked him many questions, shared information, cracked jokes, asked more questions. He was short and thin; his slick hair oozed with coconut oil, and he had a bushy drooping moustache. The white of his eyes and his teeth seemed whiter because of his dark brown skin. He smoked Charminar cigarettes incessantly.

Raju said he was a "Dalit," and then explained the meaning of the term to Abdul—someone from an "untouchable" caste. He belonged to a political organization called Dalit Panthers, and he was about to start a trade union with a friend. He worked at a textile mill. He worked for the union three days a week and asked Abdul to pick him up every day. In a few days of commuting Raju got to know everything about Abdul and told him everything about himself. Abdul noticed that for a mill worker, Raju wore expensive clothes. Raju explained earnestly, "People only take the well-dressed seriously."

From his friend Abdul received a quick lesson in the political and social history of Bombay. Raju took him around the city to different areas that made the city what it was, a microcosm of India. Abdul discovered Bombay from its myriad lanes in the old city that smelled peculiar, to its new and upcoming suburbs, which still had the look and feel of a village. Raju introduced Abdul to street food; in turn Abdul introduced Raju to Hindi movies, especially those of Amitabh Bachchan.

One day Raju took Abdul to meet a special friend.

—⁂—

That special friend was Dhinmant Desai, a young man who was working hard to start an independent trade union for Bombay's textile workers. The union office was in a chawl, a ramshackle tenement, at the intersection of Princess Street and Kalbadevi Road, behind a tonga stand. When Abdul saw Dhinmant, he wasn't impressed. He was probably in his mid-30s, his face hidden behind thick, black-framed glasses. He had piercing, large eyes, a large nose not dissimilar to Abdul's, and he was fast losing hair. Dhinmant wore a white shirt and white trousers. Abdul noticed later that he always wore white and carried a large Turkish napkin to wipe the sweat off his brow. Both he and his wife Kinnari lived and worked in the union office. Kinnari was strikingly good-looking.

With a disarming smile Dhinmant welcomed them. He put an arm around Abdul's shoulder.

"What do you do?"

"I have my taxi."

"I mean in your spare time."

Before waiting for Abdul to respond, Dhinmant asked Raju to get Abdul to the gate meeting at the mill the next evening. Abdul didn't know what a gate meeting was and asked Dhinmant.

"It is a meeting of workers at the main gate of the mill. It is generally held at the end of a shift and the beginning of another, so that a maximum number of mill workers are able to attend the meeting."

Abdul nodded uncertainly. "What do I have to do?"

"Don't let anyone disrupt the meeting. Raju will guide you."

That was Abdul's introduction to union work. It would become his life, but on that first visit he had no idea what to expect. Raju had asked many other boys to come to the gate meeting. When they reached Hans Textile Mills, where Raju worked, Dhinmant asked them to stand behind him. Abdul had expected more workers, but just about fifty assembled at the gate. To be heard, Dhinmant raised his voice. He spoke about a new concept, linking workers' wages to their output.

"The more you work, the better your productivity, the better should be your wages."

Some workers were interested, some were not, and another group shouted that it was a new way of burdening them. As if on cue, a few workers in the front rows rushed forward. Clearly, the intention was to disrupt the union meeting. Abdul grabbed one of them by the collar amid the pushing, shoving, and punching. Someone kicked Dhinmant and he fell. Raju shouted for help. Abdul fought hard with the attackers and managed to drag Dhinmant to the shade of a tree inside the mill's compound. The melee ended when a police van arrived.

"This is what I call the hard knock of life," Dhinmant said, gingerly touching his swollen forehead. "You know, I worked in this mill as an accountant for six years. I quit only recently."

"Why?"

"Long story."

That evening Dhinmant sat with them at an Irani café and spoke about his past. His grandfather had immigrated to Bombay from Dakor in Gujarat and started a textile-trading business. His father joined the business and later inherited it. The business failed, Dhinmant had to work as an accountant at the mill while he was still in college, where he met Kinnari. They were both activists and took part in demonstrations and protest marches. When he graduated from college, he continued to work at the textile mill. But both his and Kinnari's hearts were in starting a textile trade union, so Dhinmant quit his job and they started the union. Abdul left his taxi job and went to work for the union.

—⚭—

Abdul turned to glance at Ruksana. She seemed to be asleep now. He remembered a photograph from the past: Dhinmant, Raju, and he standing at the mill's gates, surrounded by hundreds of workers. Dhinmant with his left hand raised in a victory sign. The memory was so vivid in his mind, it could have happened yesterday. Later, during the 1992 violence, when the rioters set their home on fire, everything that was dear to them had burnt down, including that precious photograph.

Before that outbreak, Abdul had not been directly affected by the Hindu-Muslim communal divide. But that riot, which in reality was a pogrom, because the killing was so selective, brought home to him that however secular his outlook was, to the Hindu nationalists he would always be a Muslim, and therefore the enemy.

Ten

Abdul flicked on the light of the upstairs study and pulled out the book on computers that Ziram had brought for him from her centre and wanted him to read. He had become serious about learning to use computers after his layoff. He didn't want to stay at home, or live off his children's incomes. His layoff had been a shock. The owner of the auto shop had given no indication that he planned to sell his business and move to Florida.

"You don't have to work anymore, I make enough for all of us," Rafiq had grandly announced, when Abdul brought home the news of his layoff. Abdul hadn't felt prouder in his life than at that moment, but it wasn't an acceptable situation for him. He spoke to Kartar about working at his shop. They had both worked together briefly at Sloan Auto, but Kartar had quickly realized it was a dead end job and opened an Indian grocery shop in Toronto instead; over the years it had flourished enough for him to be able to start another shop in Brampton; these days he stayed at home, or did voluntary work at the Malton gurdwara, and his employees ran the shops for him.

"Of course," Kartar had assured him and suggested Abdul learn to use a computer so he could do billing and inventory.

As Abdul thought about his layoff, he realized that it had disrupted his life in so many ways. He had started learning to use a computer, and that had led to the discovery of Rafiq's incriminating emails from Ghani Ahmed. Though he had aged physically, he had never felt old before, but now he suddenly felt much older than his years. He turned around to glance at Ruksana. She stirred in her sleep and sat up.

"I will go down and have a glass of Eno," she said, and got out of bed.

"Chest pain?"

"Yes."

A little later, Abdul followed her downstairs. She was sitting by the kitchen window.

"How come you are not reading your holy book?"

"Saabji, the pain in my chest is spreading."

"Well, sitting won't help, pace up and down the room, and isn't it time for your namaaz?"

"No, it is too early. But how come you are so interested? You want to read the Quran and pray with me?"

"You read. I will listen, but then you will have to explain to me what you read."

His answer surprised her.

"Saabji, kya baat hai, what is the matter? How come you want to be close to Allah?"

"Once in a while that isn't such a bad thing to do, is it?" he said and grunted.

"What have you got against religion?"

"I find beliefs and rituals meaningless and useless. They blind you."

"Tauba, Saabji . . . you and your arguments. Beliefs are beliefs; they don't have to be tested."

"Ruksana, Islam prohibits idolatry but there are so many passages that describe the Prophet that one can easily frame his image in one's mind. Isn't that idolatry?"

"No, Saabji, it isn't. We are not to worship him. We are to follow his teachings."

"Excellent reply. Sometime I don't give you enough credit. All right, enough of religion. I'm hungry. You pray, I will have a bath, and make breakfast."

Ruksana knew she could easily win an argument with Abdul, answer all his doubts, but she didn't because when he began losing, he resorted to ridicule to get even, and she couldn't tolerate her belief being ridiculed. She knew her belief was not irrational. It was different from that of someone like Nagma. For Nagma religion was a crutch to fill the vacuum left in her life when her husband abandoned her. Such people eventually turned rigid and dogmatic, both in their beliefs and on their insistence on rituals. Ruksana sought tranquility in her faith.

She preferred to see the good in religion and ignore the rest, and often hoped that her husband would, too.

She brought out her prayer rug and spread it on the living room floor. She read from the Quran loudly so that Abdul could hear her. He came in with the chai and a plate full of the Indian salted butter biscuits that Kartar stocked in his store. Only Ziram liked sweet cookies; Abdul, Ruksana, and Rafiq preferred the Indian salted variety which they got from Kartar's shop.

"I think Rafiq is right to accuse us of ignoring him," Abdul mumbled, sipping his chai and nibbling at a biscuit.

"Saabji that is not true, we did whatever we could."

"He has often told me that I wasn't even in Bombay when he was born. And now that I think about it, I think he is right."

"Oh Saabji, don't be hard on yourself. Everybody works, everybody has to work."

"Yes, but I should have been more attentive to his needs. It is too late now."

They lapsed into silence.

The day Rafiq was born Abdul was in Poona for the entire month, mobilizing workers to launch an agitation to demand bonuses for the upcoming festival season. Both parents were, indeed, busy when he was born: Abdul with his trade union work, Ruksana with the women's centre and young Ziram. All the things that had seemed so important then seemed inconsequential in retrospect. They should have found time but didn't.

"I am never sure what you will say when you are in such a mood," Ruksana said.

"What do you mean?"

"Well, the next thing I know you will talk about Dhinmant. Saabji you are so wrong about Dhinmant and me."

She shouldn't have said this. Why had she done it?

"You were close to each other after Kinnari's death. I saw that."

"But not in the way you imagine."

Abdul kept quiet, but not for long. "We shouldn't have come here," he said, his voice soft, his eyes full of pain and resentment.

"You didn't like the 'Twin Towers,' remember," she said, referring to their old apartment block in Toronto.

"No, I mean we shouldn't have come to Canada."

"There was nothing left for us in India. Your home was destroyed, and you had no work."

"You wanted to leave because Dhinmant was dead."

"Nonsense. We didn't want our children to grow up in that environment, full of hatred and violence. And no prospects."

"Coming here didn't do them much good. Your daughter is married to someone a decade older and your son is in prison," Abdul said, his voice rising to a pitch.

"Saabji be quiet, they are your children."

"You live in the past, in Bombay. That is your problem, you never adjusted to Canada. Your new country was only religion. Our children may have grown up differently had you been more positive. We could all have had a different life."

He returned to the bedroom.

She sat in numb silence, neither angry nor sad. This was a routine occurrence, though the frequency of these outbursts had gone up recently. This time she had brought it on herself. She thought Dhinmant came to her mind only because he had been such a tower of strength and decisive. But so had Abdul been, there, in Bombay. She would wait for some time and then go up to be with him. Abdul had become bitter because he was lonely. Both she and he had become introverts; they couldn't make friends easily and didn't have a wide circle of friends. In India, Abdul had his trade union, in Canada there was only Kartar.

She thought of Dhinmant. Abdul was wrong about her and Dhinmant.

After she came to Bombay with Dhinmant and Kinnari, Ruksana learned typing and shorthand, and assisted Dhinmant at the union office. But she found that her heart wasn't in doing clerical work. She wanted to be out in the field, to work with the poor women of Teli Gali. One day at the community water tap, where she liked to go to get to know the women, she learned about a young woman who was set on fire and died because her family had failed to pay enough dowry to her in-laws.

Following this incident, Ruksana formed a network of women and held meetings in the afternoons in the union office. She discussed health and hygiene, but the women also wanted direct action, and devised a plan to destroy the illicit liquor den in the neighbourhood, where their husbands went to get drunk after work. Often these men came home late and became violent. There was not enough money in the home. The women informed the police of their plan and then with Ruksana they marched together and demolished the den. They faced no opposition. But Abdul was angry at Ruksana's participation. And she knew that this was because he feared for her safety. She was pleased, and knew that they were falling in love.

With this on her mind, Ruksana turned to Dhinmant one day. She knew he would give her the most reasonable advice.

"Should I marry him?"

He was aware that Ruksana and Abdul liked each other; almost everyone in Teli Gali knew that. His advice was simple: "You are alone, you want a home, and Abdul is always around, so it is natural for you to think that he is your man. But take some time to think about it a little more. Then go right ahead if you are convinced."

"So what do I do?"

"Give yourself time."

She talked Dhinmant into starting a community centre for Teli Gali's women. In six months the Mahila Kendra, the Women's Centre, became her mission in life. But Abdul was constantly on her mind, and she knew she was on his.

—⁓—

Ruksana wearily climbed the stairs up to the bedroom. Abdul had dozed off on the armchair, the computer book on his lap. She went over and slowly ruffled his hair. He opened his eyes.

"Saabji, get some sleep."

"We have been trying to avoid this for years," he said.

"What?"

"Being together, by ourselves."

From the time they met three decades ago, they had never been alone together; as the years multiplied in their married life, a compendium of hurts and resentments built up, and they instinctively began to prefer not to be alone with each other. There was so much to say, but they couldn't because that would invariably lead to arguments, and they were too tired of quarreling. Their relationship lost substance; initially they had both been dismayed at their short-lived intimacy, but they got over it. Their responsibilities as parents outweighed their differences and kept them together.

"We will manage," Ruksana said softly. "Now you try to sleep, Saabji."

Abdul held Ruksana's hand as she continued to run her fingers through his hair. "Stop, I'm going bald anyway." She led him to bed.

"Do you remember the day we decided to marry?" she said. "It was magical."

"I remember Dhinmant's starched dhoti, how uncomfortable he was," Abdul said, and guffawed.

He recalled how beautiful she was when he first saw her standing at the door of the union office. He had knocked and she had opened the door. She had a thin nose that curved at the bridge, and large eyes that formed perfect circles on her round face. She had full lips, and when she smiled two front teeth protruded, but that added to her charm because her eyes narrowed. He fell in love with her immediately. It took her some time to reciprocate.

—᠁—

With Dhinmant's union keeping him busy, Kinnari wished to follow her dream of working in the rural hinterland, where India's trade union movement had not yet reached. She moved to Nagpur to help the tobacco workers and the Adivasi indigenous populations in the countryside.

Ruksana found this strange and asked Abdul if the two were

separating. He hadn't thought about it until she brought it up, and in his usual tactless way, he put the question to Dhinmant.

"Absolutely not, we won't ever be separated," he said, laughing at the suggestion. "Kinnari is convinced that nothing less than a revolution can overthrow the fraudulent system. I don't think there can ever be a revolution in India. So she is going to work with the Adivasi people," he said.

Ruksana and Abdul were not sure how all this was linked to Kinnari's decision to work in the forests, but Abdul forbade Ruksana to raise the subject again.

One afternoon, just a couple of months later, a telegram arrived from Nagpur. Kinnari was in hospital fighting a severe bout of gastro-enteritis and malaria. By the time Dhinmant and Abdul reached her, eighteen hours later, Kinnari had died.

Ruksana was devastated. It was Kinnari who had persuaded her to come to Bombay with them. It took Dhinmant months to recover, if he did at all. He now relied on Abdul to manage the union's routine matters, and himself stayed in the office with Ruksana. A strong bond developed between them. Abdul noticed their palpable closeness and became jealous.

Eleven

Ruksana's total commitment in her fledging Women's Centre made Abdul happy. They had dinner together every evening, and talked about their work. He spoke about the union's expansion in Poona, and she about the centre and how it was growing. They didn't need excuses to be together, but they still didn't talk about the possibility of marriage.

One evening, while he was cautioning her not to be too headstrong and stubborn with the local municipality office, he gently put his hand on her shoulder and squeezed it to emphasize his point. A long awkward silence followed after he withdrew his hand. He glanced at her, then at his wristwatch, and then mumbled that he had to give his father medicine and left in a hurry. Ruksana couldn't wipe the smile off her face for a long time after he was gone.

The next day, Ruksana told Dhinmant about what had happened.

"I know he is the one. I must know whether I am the one for him," she said.

"Should I ask him?"

"Not directly."

"I know no other way."

A week later, on their way to a meeting, Dhinmant asked Abdul, "What is going on between Ruksana and you?"

Abdul shrugged his shoulders.

"Do you plan to get married?"

"It depends."

"On what?"

"Whether she wants to marry me . . . "

"Why don't you ask her?"

"What if she says no?"

"Then at least you will know. What if you don't ask and she finds someone else?"

"I won't let that happen," Abdul said, but he seemed worried.

That evening when Abdul came to the union office to have dinner with her, he hesitantly said, "Ruksana, I want to ask you something."

"What? Did something happen at the meeting today?"

"No, it is personal. About us."

She knew it was coming.

"Ruksana, have you thought of marriage?"

"Why do you ask?"

"My father has been asking me the question ever since my sister's wedding."

"So?"

"Will you?" Abdul asked.

"It is September 22, 1983 today."

"Yes. Are you saying yes or no?"

"Yes, if you promise never to leave me."

Abdul and Ruksana got married the following November. Shamsuddin, Abdul's father, was the only relative at their wedding. Abdul's sister Afraa had just given birth in Chicago, where she had moved with her husband Marzouq, and couldn't travel. Ruksana had an aunt who sent ten rupees as gift but didn't attend either. The absence of family was made up by friends. Just about everyone from Teli Gali, and Dhinmant's union, was present, and the wedding was celebrated with much fanfare. It took two days for Ruksana's henna to set on her hands. For the ceremony itself, Dhinmant wore a starched kurta that looked very uncomfortable on him, and a new dhoti. Abdul's friends formed the groom's wedding procession, the baraat, dancing to the frenzied music of the local Razak Band, which played mangled versions of wedding songs from Hindi movies.

Ruksana had wanted Abdul to sit on a horse for the procession, but he ended up preferring Dhinmant's red Maruti—another point of future contention between the two. The reception, which Dhinmant insisted on paying for, was under a makeshift canopy between the union office and Abdul's home, and the mutton biryani from Light of Asia was delicious, as expected.

That night, Shamsuddin vacated his home for the couple. The next morning, for the first time since she had come to Bombay, Ruksana slept in, missing her morning namaaz. It was close to noon when she woke. She gazed lovingly at Abdul. He was still asleep and breathing evenly. His hand was over her belly. They were two shades of brown, dark and light. He had been so tender in his lovemaking.

Ruksana remembered her parents and knew they would be happy in heaven.

A month after their wedding, Ruksana and Abdul took a week off to go to the Ajanta and Ellora caves outside Bombay. This was their belated honeymoon. During that trip Ruksana became pregnant. Dhinmant advised her to take it easy but she continued to work at the women's centre. The following October, a baby girl was born.

"She looks just like my mother," Ruksana said to Abdul.

"My father says that she actually has my mother's nose," Abdul teased.

"She will surely be a leader. Just listen to her crying," was Dhinmant's contribution to the discussion.

It was Abdul's sister Afraa who suggested they name the girl Ziram.

"What does that mean?" Abdul had asked.

"It means 'glow,'" said Afraa on the phone.

"Very appropriate," Dhinmant observed. "In our Hindu traditions, the father's sister names the newborn."

Ruksana was homebound for a month. Later, while Shamsuddin cared for Ziram at home, Abdul and Ruksana kept busy. A little over a year later, Rafiq was born, named by his grandfather, who said the boy would be "everyone's friend," as the name suggested. It was also an attribute of God.

—w—

When Shamsuddin died, not long after Rafiq's birth, Afraa came to Bombay to be with Abdul and Ruksana. She helped Abdul buy the two-room house and the union office, which the landlord was only too happy to sell.

Two deaths—Shamsuddin's and Kinnari's—brought Dhinmant and Ruksana closer. Dhinmant moved into the office after Shamsuddin's death. He didn't need the bungalow any more. Abdul was busy expanding the union's activities into other sectors and other regions beyond Bombay. He was now pretty much operating on his own. He was in Poona weekdays and returned to his home in Teli Gali for the weekends. Meanwhile Dhinmant and Ruksana spent hours together developing the women's centre that she ran.

Ruksana wanted to help the local women develop a source of income, and organized sewing classes to teach them basic skills. Through Dhinmant's contacts, sewing machines were received as donations, and in a few months the women were all trained. Again through Dhinmant's assistance, the centre obtained a contract to supply hessian bags for a cement factory.

The women had never had an independent source of income before. Dhinmant opened bank accounts for them so that they would save and not squander. Ruksana lobbied the municipal officials to start a health clinic at Teli Gali, and then urged them to cover the open gutters with cement tiles. A municipal garden was created in the neighbourhood and became a hub for families, especially during the weekends. In silent steps the complexion of Teli Gali changed.

Dhinmant's admiration for Ruksana, and her gratitude to him, grew with each success, and she became closer to him. Earlier, there had been the closeness of a patron with a charge; now they were equals. He valued her views and planned the centre's operations based on her opinions rather than his. She admired his idealism, he liked it that she agreed with most of his suggestions. She could never have had a relationship like that with Abdul, and Dhinmant couldn't have found anyone better than Ruksana to discuss his ideas with. Ruksana filled the chasm of loneliness he felt after Kinnari's death.

They would leave the house together in Dhinmant's red Maruti to go to the women's centre, and later depart for the day's appointments. They were together for nearly ten hours every day, and even when they weren't working, he came over from the union office and sat in the living room discussing the day's events.

Ruksana's success was heady and unexpected. To ease her busy schedule, Dhinmant hired a local woman to cook for them and take care of the children. But Ruksana couldn't help feeling a little guilty. She did miss Abdul and when he came for the weekends she would tell him all about her activities. Perhaps this was a defence measure. By the time Abdul was home for the weekend, her successes didn't seem that significant.

Abdul in turn missed his family wherever he was. He lived in a rented house on the outskirts of Poona. Ruksana wanted him to return to Bombay, but he didn't want Dhinmant to think that he was shirking his responsibilities. He had noticed the new closeness between his wife and his mentor. He was alarmed, when he saw them, at how they anticipated each other's responses, and seemed to know what the other was thinking. He was envious and felt neglected, but didn't know what to say to Ruksana. He didn't want to appear petty, and she was oblivious of his discomfort. Abdul's behaviour changed gradually. He turned a little distant with everybody.

Dhinmant perceived the change.

"Is something wrong?" he asked one day.

"No, why do you ask?"

"You seem very formal nowadays."

"I haven't been able to find time for Ruksana and the kids."

"Let Raju handle Poona, you come back."

Abdul jumped at the proposal. Ruksana was happy too; she had no cause to feel guilty now. She had made a long list of things that she and Abdul and the kids would do together. On top of the list was Ziram's admission to kindergarten. In Abdul's absence, it would have been Dhinmant who would have come with her.

III

A Walk in the Rain

.

Twelve

Jameel was unwilling to offer any advice to Ziram's family, but he was eager and willing to help. Rafiq's arrest had unnerved him, pushed him into a role he wasn't sure he wanted to take on. He was an outsider to the family, had always been one, and preferred to remain that way, but now suddenly he was forced to get involved. He was from Trinidad, his grandparents having been indentured labourers from India. That was some century and a half ago, and he felt disconnected from there.

He couldn't share the culture or language with his in-laws, and sometimes even with Ziram, and although he could make the odd reference to some old Hindi films, it was not the same. He was the stranger. He spoke in a different accent, his childhood memories were different, and even his sense of humour. He was not brought up religious either, but for the sake of the family he had given up—almost—his partiality to rum.

With this new development, he tried hard to bridge his distance from them, and attempted to show that he cared. He did this in different ways—with an understanding word or two, helping Abdul fill out the forms that Anita had sent, cutting French beans for Ruksana.

Ziram's parents found this extra attention somewhat bothersome and confusing. They did not know how to respond, weren't sure the concern was genuine, or that he really understood them. But Ziram was grateful to him, and that mattered. She was happy that he hadn't spoken up about the possible damage to his promotion because of her brother's stupidity. She would feel guilty and responsible forever, if that happened, even though she knew that Jameel would never blame her or her family. He was too much of a gentleman. She realized that his excessive fussing over her pregnancy was a manifestation of his worry.

Staying at her parents' townhouse was turning out to be stressful for them both; she was surprised and unhappy about that. She had always felt that after she and Jameel moved into their apartment, she hadn't been able to spend enough time with her parents. But now, having been with them for the last few days, she realized that she was finding it difficult to adjust; it was all quite suffocating. Jameel was feeling no different, but he wouldn't suggest that they return to their apartment. It had to come from her. Finally, when she couldn't stand the stress any longer, she decided to talk to her parents.

It was at the breakfast table. Ziram's voice was unsteady, she wasn't sure of their reaction. "Abba, we've been thinking about all this . . . " she began, then faltered, and looked at Jameel for support, but he wasn't willing to bail her out. "It'd be better if we moved back to our apartment," she finally came out, her voice quavering.

"But Beta we need you . . . " Ruksana responded immediately.

Abdul interrupted her. He agreed with Ziram. A couple needed their privacy. "No, you are right, Ziram. How long can you be here?"

"I'm extending my leave, I'll be here every day, and we'll be with you at the court for the bail hearing," Ziram said, immensely relieved.

Ruksana lapsed into silence, then said, "Look after yourself in your condition. And remember, your brother isn't bad."

"I know," Ziram said, already feeling guilty.

"Why doesn't anyone ever think of what I want?" Ruksana said bitterly after they left.

Abdul put a hand on his wife's shoulder and gently squeezed it.

—⁓—

As they drove to their apartment, Ziram was thinking about Jameel's promotion. "Call up Mike and ask him if he can help you," she said. Mike was their senior colleague and often helped people out. She knew he liked them, and he liked her especially, to the point of sometimes flirting with her. He had helped to get her in at the centre as an intern, and later orchestrated her appointment to a permanent position.

"I'll call from home and tell him that I'm taking the day off, and I'll also tell him about extending your leave," Jameel said.

"Talk specifically about the promotion."

"Yeah, OK. Relax now."

They reached home, hoping they would be able to relax, but that wasn't easy because he was worried and preoccupied with missing an opportunity, and she was feeling guilty that she had abandoned her parents. Jameel called the centre, but Mike didn't answer, so he left a voice message. Ziram began to cook lunch, and put on a DVD to take her mind off Rafiq and her parents.

Unlike her mother and her husband, for whom cooking was a passion, for Ziram it was a chore. Jameel took charge of the kitchen once a month and created heavenly fish recipes, though for days afterward, her hair smelled of fish, and even after a thorough shampoo the feral cat that sauntered around their workplace would hover around her cubicle.

She wanted to ask Jameel to help her in the kitchen but didn't. It was better that he relax. They had a quiet lunch. The Hindi movie on the DVD made enough noise to cover their gloomy silence. A tear rolled down her cheek. Jameel looked at her, and came to her. He wiped the tear, and gently took her in his arms.

"Go change; let's go to bed," he said.

She came out wearing her "jammies"—a light blue shirt with dark blue satin lace on the sleeves and collars. The pyjamas also had lace running along the side. He couldn't understand why a grown woman would want to wear clothes more suited to a little girl, but he liked them on her. She knew the effect they had on him. His eyes widened at the sight of her cleavage, and at how her hips stretched the fabric. Their marriage was still young.

She had inherited her mother's looks: the same thin nose that curved at the bridge and the same large eyes and round face. But it was her slight plumpness that excited Jameel. She glanced in the mirror and rubbed her hand on her belly—it was already ballooning softly. She wondered if it would be a boy or a girl. She wanted a girl.

After nearly a week of self-imposed restriction at her parents' place, both needed each other. They made love unhurriedly and passionately.

"You better call Mike now," Ziram said.

Jameel got up, walked to the living room and called Mike again.

This time Mike answered. Jameel told him about taking the day off, and about extending Ziram's leave by a couple of days. He asked Mike if Rafiq's arrest would have a negative impact on his promotion. Mike's response was uncertain: "I don't think so; but who knows?"

Jameel returned to bed; he wasn't going to go crazy over the promotion. He knew he deserved it more than anyone else, but if he didn't get it, he was prepared to look for other avenues.

"I've no idea why Rafiq did all this," Ziram said, snuggling up to him.

"Something that we don't know, and can't comprehend," he replied.

"I think 9/11 changed him. He was beaten up at school and humiliated," she said, biting her lips thoughtfully.

Jameel gently rubbed his hand over her stomach.

"But that doesn't lead to all this."

"Well, it made me aware of my identity as a Muslim. It wasn't about race, it was only about religion. Even people with the same skin colour as mine saw me differently because I was a Muslim. For the first time, I understood my parents' nightmare in India during the riots."

"You know, 9/11 affected Muslims everywhere, especially here in the West, but we all found ways to cope. My mother faced discrimination at work but she fought back. Everyone faces some discrimination in Canada, but that doesn't turn them into fanatics," Jameel said.

"Abba and Ammi reacted as if it was their fate. They should've complained when Rafiq was bullied and beaten up at school, but they accepted it passively, and forced him to be passive, too," Ziram said. Then, after a pause, she added, "I'm sure that must've have radicalized Rafiq."

Jameel agreed with her but only to an extent. He didn't want to stir up a debate, so kept his thoughts to himself. He agreed that a young mind couldn't but be scarred by such prejudice. To feel victimized was one thing, but to join hands with the likes of Ghani Ahmed was to go to an extreme. He was tired and—despite Rafiq, and his own promotion prospects hanging in the balance—happy to be home and in their bed. He dozed off. She gazed at him, and moved her fingers through the hair on his chest. Jameel opened his eyes briefly, smiled, and went back to sleep.

The telephone rang, and Ziram answered it instantly, not wanting to disturb Jameel. She groaned when she heard Nagma Khala.

"I am not disturbing you, I hope," Nagma said, sounding upset. "I called your Ammi but she isn't answering."

"No, no . . . that is OK," Ziram replied, not knowing what to say. It always took two or three sentences before Ziram could follow Nagma's Dekhani Hindustani, peppered as it always was with strange expressions.

"Beta you all better be careful. I have heard that the police may implicate you."

"What do you mean?"

"The police came, asked me questions about the crèche, and our new centre."

"What did they ask?" Ziram asked, curious but apprehensive.

"They wanted to know what I teach the children at my crèche. I said I narrate stories from Islam about our Prophet."

"And?" Ziram asked impatiently. This Indian habit of going round and round and not coming straight to the point always irritated her.

"They asked me about my husband. I told them I had no idea where he is, for all I care the bastard may as well be dead. They asked me how many of these boys I knew."

"What boys?"

"They told me several boys were arrested. They are arresting these kids for petty things."

"Khala, they were planning mass murders. That is not petty." Ziram was making an effort to keep her voice low; she wanted to shout in exasperation.

"Beta, who knows? I have heard one of them was arrested merely because he was looking at some maps on the computer."

The conversation was alarming Ziram. Either Nagma Khala had ice in her veins, or she was complicit in the conspiracy. "Khala do you know all of them?"

"No, but I wish I did," Nagma said.

"Khala, did Rafiq ever speak to you about Ghani Ahmed?"

"Yes, and I told him that not everyone approved of what that man was planning."

Ziram was shocked. "You knew about Ghani Ahmed's plans, and you kept quiet?"

"I didn't approve of what they were planning, because Islam doesn't preach or condone massacre of innocent people in its name."

"This doesn't make any sense. Why did you keep quiet?" Ziram asked, her voice rising.

"These kids were merely trying to make people aware of what is going on in our world."

"By mass murder? Do you even realize what you're saying? You're insane!" Ziram exclaimed, but then lowered her voice when she saw Jameel stir in sleep.

"His life is ruined now. I wish he had married that Gujarati girl," Nagma said with a sigh.

"You knew about that?" Ziram asked.

"He told me about her, but at that time he was too young. What was her name . . . ?"

But Ziram didn't want to talk to her. She found Nagma Khala's ambiguity alarming and morally unacceptable. The woman didn't sound either ashamed or disturbed. Ziram wondered whether every Muslim thought as Nagma Khala did, or whether the old woman was an odd one.

Ziram wasn't willing to accept that Nagma's opinions represented what most Muslims thought, but she also knew that her own family's liberal ideas weren't popular either. She had always felt that her parents were a bunch of idealistic misfits—and she knew that they had been misfits even in India. But she was happy to share their idealism.

She had been distinctly lucky to have found Jameel. With him, whatever adjustments she had had to make in her thinking were generally more liberal than what she was conditioned to think by her upbringing. She and her husband didn't pray or read the Quran—though she had been taught it. During Ramzan she fasted at most a couple of days, he never. And although he didn't know it, she was aware that in company he indulged in a little alcohol. And yet they were Muslims.

—\~\~—

Ziram would never admit it, but she admired Jameel more than she loved him. She had chosen right, she couldn't possibly have found anyone better than him. He was caring and gentle. He had encouraged her to step out of her confines—some self-imposed, some circumstantial. He had given her the freedom to think for herself, to find herself and become the person she had always wanted to be.

Jameel had been one of her teachers at Sheridan College in Brampton. She had joined Sheridan while she was engaged to her cousin Azam, but had dropped out after Azam was killed in a car crash. She had rejoined the college to take her mind off the tragedy, and had no intention of hooking up with anyone. Initially, she found Jameel intimidating, and she had resolved to avoid him. He spoke with a slight musical accent because he was born in Trinidad. He was unusually tall. His high cheekbones, distinct jawline, and tall forehead made his face seem square. He had a thin, narrow nose and thin lips. His eyes were deep set and his hair was already turning a distinguished grey.

"You can't dodge fate," he had said later, when she told him that she couldn't have imagined marrying him.

One afternoon, Ziram borrowed a book on substance abuse from the library for her assignment, and queued up at a cafeteria inside the college campus for tea. She heard a man clearing his throat, and when she turned around she saw Jameel behind her. When she ordered her usual tea, the server said, "We don't have your English Breakfast."

"Try Earl Grey, without milk or sugar," Jameel suggested.

She wasn't sure, because his voice sounded hard. But the smile was disarming and warm. She ordered as he suggested. The man behind the counter got their teas.

"All together?" he asked, and she nodded uncertainly and paid for both. Jameel handed her a toonie as they walked away from the counter.

"Do you mind if I have tea with you?" he asked but obviously didn't expect any answer, because he sat down on a bench opposite her before she could reply. His gaze unnerved her. She didn't know what to talk about, and apparently neither did he, at least initially. Then he began to talk about the program she was in, and she was relieved for the awkward silence to be broken. He drew her out slowly, even if he was no great conversationalist himself.

After Azam's death, she had locked herself away from the world for a long time and had preferred to be alone. Although Jameel was no more than a stranger, she felt better talking to him. She met him in the class every day, and they nodded at each other briefly, occasionally exchanging a smile. He was a good teacher, even if—unusually for a teacher—a man of not many words. Then in winter, as she was waiting at the bus stop outside the campus, he was driving by and stopped. He asked her to get in. She hesitated for a moment, and then got in; it was better than waiting in the cold for the bus.

"I'm going to Toronto, I can drop you home. Do you live in Brampton?" he asked. Again, his intense gaze unsettled her.

She shook her head. The car had a tangy lime smell.

"Toronto. Caledonia and Lawrence," she said softly.

"That's great, I'll have company all the way," he said, trying hard to sound friendly. "I'm at Dufferin and St. Clair."

It was dark outside and he drove carefully. Everything about this man was measured, nothing spontaneous at all. He was like her father, but totally different from Azam. Of course, his decision to halt his car at the bus stop to give her a ride had to be spontaneous. Ziram was feeling good being with him, just as she had been while having tea with him. In about a week, he was driving her to school and back home every day, and she would catch him gazing at her intently before turning away to watch the road.

He told her his day job was at the Malton Settlement and Community Centre, and he taught at Sheridan College so that he could be occupied in the evenings after work. She liked him because he was everything that she wanted in a man. But she knew she didn't love him. After Azam went away from her life, she could never fall in love again.

Slowly, she managed to piece together his story. His parents were now in Vancouver, and had been there for many years. He had done a master's degree in social work followed by a fairly long stint in Trinidad, where he assisted a local NGO to start a microcredit scheme in a large slum. Within a few months Ziram had made up her mind that even if she couldn't love again, she would marry Jameel. She spoke to him about it, and he agreed immediately.

"Yes of course. And thank you for asking. I would've taken a few years to get around to doing so," he said, unable to hide his elation.

She didn't want to announce her decision to her parents; rather, she wanted to involve them in it. So she hinted about it obliquely to her mother. Ziram knew Ammi would tell Abba. One day she brought Jameel home. She was surprised that her parents were pleased, and didn't seem to mind that he was at least a decade older than her. But her parents' "typically Indian attitude" still never failed to irritate Ziram. After he left, Ruksana couldn't help exclaiming, "Kala—how dark he is. But he's a good man, nevertheless." Ziram shook her head and mumbled to herself, "Still so fucking caught up with skin colour."

Jameel's interest in her and her family had also intensified when he learned that Ziram's Abba and Ammi had been activists in Bombay. In their turn, they too began to look at Jameel differently. "Oh, an activist—he is one of us," her mother exclaimed when she came to know of his work in slums. After Ziram completed her program at Sheridan, Jameel spoke to Mike and invited her to do an internship at the centre.

Thirteen

Ziram had loved Azam, she still did. Whenever he came to mind her belief in God and her tenuous faith in natural justice completely evaporated. The two of them were to be married after his MBA program at Loyola University in Chicago. He was Abba's sister Afraa's son, and just a year older. Although Abba and Ammi had disapproved of the match at first, they relented when they saw how determined Ziram and Azam were about their future together.

The relationship began during a trip to Bombay. Such things happened in the movies when a boy and a girl walked in the rain, and kissed; at least that is what she was told. She had heard her parents say, during their far-too-frequent reminiscences about their "Bambai," that a couple had merely to walk in Bombay's downpour along Marine Drive to become inseparable for the rest of their lives. Consequently, when it happened to her, she wasn't surprised at all.

Ruksana had always been keen to return to India for a short visit. She knew they couldn't afford it, but their Teli Gali neighbours in Bombay had been inviting her for a long time. It sounded tempting. Abdul, always thrifty, was not willing to throw away money on a purposeless trip. He suggested she take the kids to visit his sister Afraa in Chicago; it turned out she was planning a trip to India that summer to attend a wedding, and she suggested they accompany her and Azam.

Abdul had no choice but to borrow money from his employer and sent his family to India for three weeks. Afraa and Ruksana met at Heathrow en route after nearly two decades. They nearly brought everything at the airport lounge to a stop with their hysterical hugging and bawling. There was a lot of catching up to do. They abandoned their heavily accented English for rapid-fire Bambaiya dialect, that peculiar mixture of several languages and dialects, with a dash of slang.

"Ammi, everyone's looking," Ziram whispered. She and Azam,

whom she'd just met, exchanged embarrassed glances, then shrugged their shoulders. Rafiq thought his mother had gone crazy.

Their cousin had a scraggly beard, fuzzy overgrown hair up to his shoulders, and acne. He was chewing gum without pause and was wearing large earphones connected to a portable CD player. In a red t-shirt with the iconic silhouette of Che Guevara in the front, he was obviously trying hard to look cool, but only managed to look gawky. Ziram was in love nonetheless.

They sat together on the flight to Bombay and talked about their school, their homes, their friends and parents, everything they could think of. It was past midnight when they reached Bombay.

—ɷ—

Ziram and Azam were curious about Bombay, but they didn't know that summer in North America was the monsoon season in India. Their mothers, however, who had an intimate relationship with the city's weather, were looking forward to the rains.

"What is this?" Azam asked his mother, peering through the window of their hotel room, the next morning. He had never seen such a waterfall before.

"Bambai ki barish!—This is the famous Bombay monsoon. Nothing in the world can match its glory," Afraa exclaimed, clapping her hands in glee, as she pulled the curtains back to see the downpour.

Her son found that way too dramatic. She was ready to go to Teli Gali, where she had grown up with Abdul, and wanted him to come along. But he wasn't going anywhere in this weather. In the other room, Ruksana was ready to leave with Rafiq. Ziram had taken ill. Afraa wrote a phone number of their old neighbour in Teli Gali, and told Azam, "If Ziram needs anything, call us."

Azam switched on the TV and flipped through the channels—most of the shows were Hindi movies or songs. He loved Hindi movies because he had been raised on a steady diet of Hindi cinema, but now he was bored. On the news channel, he saw that the rains had brought Bombay to a halt. Suburban trains had stopped in their tracks, and the streets, swollen with rainwater and choked with traffic, had the appearance of a long, fat python in a narrow river. He wanted to knock on Ziram's door, but wasn't sure whether she was awake.

It was she who got to him first. He was still in his pyjamas but quickly opened the door. Ziram was wearing a gown, which both their mothers called a nightie.

"I'm bored," she said and walked in. She sat on a chair near the window and looked outside. "This is crazy and beautiful," she said, looking out the window. "Our room doesn't have the street view."

She sat beside him, smelling of toothpaste and soap. He tried not to stare at her cleavage. He was suddenly conscious of his own body odour but she didn't seem to notice or care.

"Let's go out?" Ziram said.

"In this weather? Are you fucking crazy?"

"We can go to Marine Drive, and walk by the sea. Abba and Ammi often talk about how the waves surge, and spill over on the sidewalks, drenching everyone and everything. I want to go there, see that," she said, grabbing his hands and pulling him to the window. "Have you seen anything like this?"

He clearly hadn't, and getting wet in the rain wasn't his idea of fun; but he liked the idea of going out with her.

"I'll change into my jeans and a shirt. You get ready," she said.

Ziram told the cabbie to take them to Marine Drive, and bring them back. "We're going to see the waves," she said in a mixture of English and Hindustani.

"You should walk from Chowpatty to Nariman Point, that is where the waves are the tallest," the taxi driver said, nodding sagely.

Ten minutes into the taxi ride, the magic of the Bombay rains enveloped them. It was at once majestic and mystifying. Raindrops hit the car roof like a million pellets. Both of them peered out of the windows, rubbing the fog to clear the glass. It took more than two hours to reach Marine Drive, and it rained incessantly all the way. At Chowpatty, they got out and walked. The taxi driver, realizing these were crazy NRI— foreign-Indian—kids, didn't have the heart to cheat them. He suggested he would meet them down the road at the Churchgate intersection.

"This is awesome," Ziram said.

"We should've got an umbrella," Azam replied, frowning. He had become drenched almost as soon as he got off the cab.

"Who needs an umbrella? This is so much fun," Ziram said, holding his hand, and merrily swinging it.

Her smile was infectious, and soon he was smiling, too. They were soaked to their bones, and the rain felt like a whiplash on their backs. To their right, the dark horizon was a smudge and it was impossible to distinguish where the dark sea began and the overcast sky ended. The sea rose in anger and crashed into the sidewalk with a ferocity that was both frightening and exhilarating. They weren't alone, there were many couples sharing this magic. And to their left there was wild honking from the cars as the traffic crawled.

Suddenly, Azam began to run. Ziram followed, a few steps behind him, and when she caught up with him, breathless, she asked him to stop. He held her in his arms, and she made no attempt to move away.

"We're on one of Bombay's busiest roads," Ziram said, as she held his arm. They walked holding each other, smiling, giggling, and laughing.

When they reached the intersection, both were hungry. Azam wanted to sit somewhere, because he was shivering; but it had more to do with the excitement of being in close proximity to this beautiful, charming girl, and less with his wet clothes. They shared a pizza, and then held hands in the cab, going back. She gazed into his eyes. He kissed her.

"You'll have to shave off the beard," she said, sounding very serious.

"Why and when?"

"You idiot, when we get married, because it tickles me!"

"What makes you think we will?"

Ziram pulled hard at his beard and he yelled in pain.

—⁓—

In the hotel room, Ruksana chatted on the phone, scheduling more meetings for the next day. She was shocked when she saw her daughter.

Ziram's clothes were soaking, her hair dishevelled.

"Where did you go?"

"To Marine Drive . . . "

"This isn't Toronto . . . it isn't safe," Ruksana said. She was annoyed that Ziram had gone out with Azam but wasn't sure what to say. "You are coming with us tomorrow."

"No, Ammi. I won't."

—⁓—

Ziram had made her own plans with Azam. Ruksana spoke to Afraa, and tried to explain that Azam and Ziram were of the wrong age to be together. Afraa suggested Rafiq go with them. Ruksana wasn't entirely happy with the solution but agreed.

A day before Azam and Afraa were to leave for the wedding in Poona, Ziram suggested to Azam that they go for a swim in the hotel pool. He bought swimwear for them both from one of the shops in the lobby. Rafiq didn't want to enter the pool because, he declared, "the water is contaminated." Ziram and Azam were in the pool for hours. They didn't want to come out of the water, but had to because Rafiq began to moan loudly that he was hungry.

Ziram changed into shorts and a t-shirt and smiled to herself. Ammi wouldn't have approved of her clothes. After Rafiq fell asleep, Ziram tiptoed out, and knocked on Azam's door. He opened it immediately, a towel wrapped around his waist, his body still wet from the shower. He grabbed her before she closed the door. His hands were all over her. Azam led her to the bed and pulled her over him. He kissed her and clutched at her breasts, he grabbed her buttocks tightly. She shook the towel from his waist, and grabbed his penis. It felt alive in her hand, throbbing, pulsating. Passionate but inexperienced, their lovemaking was furtive, painful and brief.

—⁓—

Ziram knew her mother would throw a melodramatic fit if she got wind of her relationship with Azam, so she instructed him to keep quiet about it during his Poona trip. But Ruksana could see her daughter was anxious. She waited for Afraa and Azam to leave.

"What is going on?" she asked, the minute Afraa and Azam left the hotel in a taxi.

"Ammi, can we talk about this later?"

"You are in love with that boy," the mother said accusingly.

Ziram wasn't surprised her mother had understood her feelings for Azam; she had a knack for such things. "Are you mad at me?"

"You will hurt yourself more if you don't stop," Ruksana said.

"Ammi, I can't help it."

A similar drama unfolded on the taxi to Poona a little later. All Afraa could manage to say when she heard of her son's love for her niece was to call him bewakoof, an idiot, and slap her hand to her forehead. On their flight back home, three days later, the mothers discussed all kinds of options and scenarios, and hoped that once they got busy with their lives, the young people would forget their monsoon interlude.

Separation only intensified their ardour. They chatted for hours on the internet, exchanged emails, and talked on the phone. Their mothers could do nothing to stop them; and Ziram and Azam were street smart enough not to let their dads know. When Ziram finished high school and Azam graduated, they told their respective dads. To their surprise, they were neither surprised nor opposed to the idea, but they wanted them to study further first. Abdul wanted Ziram to go to college, and Marzouq wanted Azam to do his MBA.

"But that'll take too long," Ziram protested, when Azam told her about his dad's advice.

"He thinks we need that time."

"Then we'll get engaged," she insisted.

Though not a custom, everyone agreed that a betrothal was the best solution. Azam came with his parents to Toronto, and the couple exchanged rings in a simple ceremony. Ziram enrolled at Sheridan College in Brampton for a social work degree. Azam started his MBA in Chicago. He frequently came to Toronto, and they spent weekends together. Both worked part-time.

Then the tragedy happened.

—⁂—

One morning in Chicago while Azam was driving to college, a speeding truck rammed into him. He died on the spot.

Ziram's world collapsed. Everything that she had planned for in her life had Azam in it. Now she didn't know what to do. Her parents were worried she might do something drastic. But after six months of grieving at home in seclusion from the world, she realized that she had to get out of her depression. She learned from her mother that Azam's parents had left Chicago and settled in New Jersey. This was a further cue that she too should move on in life. Her best option was to return to school. Eventually everything worked out just fine, she met Jameel, and within a couple of years after Azam's death, she was married. Ziram told Jameel everything about Azam. For her that was the only way she could put those memories to rest. He was kind and understanding.

In return, she asked if there had been another woman in his life. There had to be, but she wanted to hear that from him.

"Yes, long ago," Jameel had said.

He met her during his first trip to Port of Spain in Trinidad, and she had been the reason he had stayed in Port of Spain for six years. He had returned to Canada when things didn't work out between them. It wasn't easy to resettle, and it took a long time for him to find a proper job. Most of his friends from school and university had moved on, and his colleagues at the centre were now his friends. His parents had moved to Vancouver.

—⁂—

Life evens out, Ziram thought. At least it had evened out for her, but it hadn't for Ammi and Abba. They had suffered, and suffered long. And now, this thing with Rafiq. She didn't want to add to their suffering. After a few fitful hours of sleep, she was up again the next morning. Jameel had slept through most of the day and night.

"Drop me home before going to work," she told Jameel.

"If that's home, what's this?" he asked, and smiled.

"Heaven," she said, smiling back.

When they arrived at her parents' house, Ammi was sitting on her prayer mat, reading her holy book. Abba was lying on his side on the couch watching TV, the sound muted.

"Any news?" Jameel asked his father-in-law.

"Anita called last evening. The bail hearing is tomorrow. We have to be at the courthouse in the morning," Abdul spoke wearily.

"So, it'll all be decided tomorrow?" Ziram asked.

"Only the bail part," Ruksana said. "Only Allah knows what will happen afterwards."

Fourteen

Rafiq had been in an isolation cell at the Maplehurst detention centre in Milton for over a week. His routine comprised of breakfast, shower, walk in the yard, lunch, staring at the wall, prayers, reading from the Quran, more staring at the wall, early supper, and a restless night in bed. Breakfast was two blueberry muffins, a couple of chocolate chip cookies, and a small carton of plain milk. He avoided meat because he wasn't sure if it was halal. After breakfast, he waited his turn to shower along with the other prisoners.

After his first morning, he had avoided taking a shower for a couple of days. He had been dumbfounded by the sight of naked men in various sizes and shapes taking showers together without the slightest embarrassment. When, finally, feeling too dirty, he showed up for a shower after a couple of days, the officer who had noticed his discomfort earlier remarked sarcastically, "Ready to drool over asses again?" There was laughter all around and bawdy remarks and slapping of thighs. Some of the men touched each other.

He had been told that a shower was a dangerous place for young men in prison. He was terrified of being attacked. He was the youngest, and the only brown man there. He realized how prison could change a man for ever. Talking idealism and revenge was one thing, but he had never bargained for this.

After his quick showers, braving the chill, he spent some time in the yard for a bit of sunlight; after that he had nothing to do. There was no computer and there were no books, and so he immersed himself into the holy book, and he prayed.

He would repeatedly read his favourite verses from the Quran, and recite from memory his most favourite lines:

There is no God save Him, the Living, the Eternal.
Slumber never overtakes Him, nor does sleep weary Him.

Unto Him belong all things in Heaven and on the earth.
Who shall intercede with Him save by His will?
He knows what is before and what comes after,
And no man can comprehend whatsoever save by His will.
His Throne is as vast as the Heavens and the earth,
And the keeping of them does not wear Him.
He is the exalted, the Mighty One.

—⟳—

Rafiq discovered the difference between solitude and loneliness. It was a puzzle: when he was in the midst of people, he preferred to be alone, and now when he was all alone, he needed people desperately. He missed his family, missed Ammi's constant monitoring of his movements and activities, Ziram's blunt opinions, Abba's cryptic remarks, Nagma Khala's doting indulgences. He missed Wanderlust, his place of work. He tried not to think of Stacey, his colleague and boss's young wife at Wanderlust, who would tease him with her ways, bending over him to expose her breasts or crossing her legs from afar. Sometimes the thought of her gave him a wet dream.

Generally he kept to himself. That seemed to be the norm. Except for the bawdy jokes in the shower, and some bantering with an officer, there was little interaction between prisoners. Most of them seemed preoccupied with their own thoughts, ignoring everyone and everything else. He tried to smile at some of the older prisoners, expecting sympathy, but they ignored him. One particularly grumpy prisoner showed him the finger every day in the yard and shouted "*ārlaulības bērns.*" He said that to everyone; Rafiq had no idea what that meant, and it seemed that nobody else did.

A few days into his detention, a tall, lanky inmate, with the haggard look of an alcoholic, his mouth reeking of cigarettes, stopped in front of him in the yard. Rafiq looked up at the looming character.

"Hey, Sand Nigger, you tried to blow up the city?" the guy asked.

Rafiq turned away and instead looked down at his shoes. The man pushed him hard, and he fell down. An officer came over to intercede.

He offered a hand to Rafiq and helped him get up.

"Lay off, Eliot," the officer said, and the man walked away laughing. He joined a group of other prisoners at the other end of the yard near the high wall. The officer then turned to Rafiq, and said: "Go to your cell, kid, and take care. These guys are a bunch of lunatics."

"Thanks," Rafiq said.

"I'm Shawn," the officer said, and offered his hand again. Rafiq shook it limply, looked at him warily, and when he saw him smiling, felt reassured for the first time since his arrest. He tried to smile back, but had to fight back a sob.

"I wanted to stretch my arms and legs for a bit," he said, "Gets tiresome inside the cell."

Shawn nodded and walked away. Rafiq cautiously looked towards Eliot and his group. As though anticipating his look, they stared at him menacingly. He continued to walk at the other end, where he was, as far away from them as possible. How long was this ordeal going to last? He would do anything to get out, he thought. But what could he do? Suppose he was sentenced for years? He would hang himself. That was a sin.

"Hey Sand Nigger, get over here," Eliot hollered when Shawn had gone inside the building. The group of men laughed loudly, slapping each other on their backs, and pointing at him. They broke into a chicken dance. Rafiq was angry, scared, and humiliated, but he knew it was pointless to complain much. He was furious with himself that they could intimidate him so easily. But he was not made like them, all hardened criminals. I come from a respectable family. I am a softy.

Later that morning, another guard came to his cell. "Officers here to talk to you," he said curtly and led him to a room just behind the visitors' lounge. This room was different from the one in which he had met Anita. This was a bigger, better room. It had leather furniture—couch and chairs, a table. There was also a work desk at the right of the rectangle room. The room was brightly lit. Two men sat on a leather couch which was placed against the far wall. Both wore suits and gave off the clean odour of cologne. One of them was lean with a narrow face and had a valise on his lap.

"Hello, Rafiq, I'm Eric," he said. "And this is Jeff." Jeff gave a nod. "We are from the Canadian Security Intelligence Service. You heard of it? We are here to ask you a few questions."

Rafiq stared wide-eyed at them. He had expected them to be brusque as everyone here had been. Their affability bothered him. What lay behind it? He was afraid of CSIS's involvement because he had read about the torture of prisoners in Guantanamo Bay, and even here in Canada. Were they going to torture him? Hand him over to the Americans? Would he disappear?

Eric stood up, proffering a hand. Rafiq mistook the gesture and thought the officer was about to hit him. He lurched backward and almost fell over.

"Easy . . . sit down," Eric said and pulled him by the hand before he fell.

Rafiq sat down on one of two upright chairs and glanced furtively at his two interrogators.

Jeff had remained sitting, his eyes all the time on Rafiq, sizing him up. He had a clean-shaven head and large round eyes with the crooked nose of a boxer. Eric had icy blue eyes.

Eric gave a studied look at Rafiq. After some moments he said, "You came to Canada in 1994?"

Fear was hampering comprehension. Rafiq was still so scared that at first he didn't quite catch the question and stared at them blankly. Eric repeated the question. These are CSIS guys, Rafiq said to himself; don't say anything that would cause more problems, a voice inside warned him. But if he didn't . . . He stifled a sob and gulped. Instinctively he covered his ears with his hands and tightly shut his eyes.

From afar, he heard Jeff say, "We're here to get some answers, so you better talk, Rafiq." He knew it was Jeff because the voice was different.

In a gentler voice, Eric asked, "You came to Canada in 1994?"

Rafiq gave a little nod and said: "Y . . . yes."

"Who helped your family leave India?" Eric asked.

"I . . . I don't know."

"Think," Jeff urged.

"I . . . I really don't know," Rafiq said, his voice still small.

"Did your mother work as a security guard?" Eric asked.

"Yes."

"Kartar Grewal came here in 1974. Did he know your father in India?" Eric asked.

"I don't know."

"Who funded your family's trip to Canada?"

"My father sold our home and his ancestral property," Rafiq replied quickly. This made him a little more confident.

"You went to an Islamic daycare centre?" Eric asked, the question more a statement.

"It wasn't Islamic . . . " Rafiq said and then abruptly changed his mind. "I mean, yes." He figured that these men might go away if he gave them the answers they expected. He wanted his ordeal to end. He would even make up the answers, he thought.

"The woman who owns the place is Nagma Khan?" Eric asked.

"Yes."

"Who's her husband?" Jeff asked.

"I don't know," Rafiq said.

"How can you not know that? You work with her, don't you? Do you know what a sleeper cell is?" Eric asked.

"Yes."

It dawned upon Rafiq that these officers might be trying to frame Nagma Khala and his family by linking them to Ghani Ahmed.

"My family isn't involved, they had nothing to do with all this," Rafiq stated forcefully. "They didn't know anything about what I was doing, and I didn't do anything either. All I did was exchange a few emails."

He awaited their reaction.

"Your recorded statement says you did reconnaissance," Jeff said calmly, after a studied pause.

"Yes, but nothing more."

"That's not true. You were sent to Kathmandu for weapons training," Jeff said, raising his voice slightly.

This was news to him. Rafiq gaped at the two officers. He had been deluded into believing that the Kathmandu trip was for him to go to a religious camp.

Then, rather abruptly, Jeff asked, "Did you meet Abu Hafiz in Kathmandu?"

"Did you, Rafiq?" Eric pressed.

" . . . no . . . " Rafiq mumbled.

"He didn't come to Kathmandu, do you know why?" Jeff asked.

"I don't know . . . who is Abu Haa . . . ?"

"Hafiz. Then you went to India," Eric said.

"Ahmedabad . . . it was at the height of summer, like some 40 degrees in the shade, I got sunstroke, and had to be rushed to the hospital . . . I flew back in a couple of days."

"You had weapons training in Kathmandu," Eric asked.

"My Kathmandu visit had nothing to do with all this. I was there to attend a religious camp."

"It was a weapons and IED training camp," Jeff said.

Rafiq looked at them, bewildered. He had done nothing wrong during that trip. The two CSIS men asked more questions, but now these were mostly commonplace, not related to his emails and his arrest. His fear abated as he was asked about his growing up years, his family, and their struggles. Then suddenly the session ended, and the two men stood up.

"We're done for now," Eric said.

—m—

Rafiq lay awake in his cell. The interrogation hadn't gone the way he had expected. The questions intrigued him, confused him. The interrogators had not followed any pattern, and it had seemed that they were asked merely to corroborate what CSIS already knew. Jeff and Eric had known about his trip to Nepal and India. He had been under the assumption, obviously erroneous as he was discovering now, that it was a religious camp he was being sent to, when it was for weapons training that he had been sent to Nepal. But then, if the cops knew this much, he was sure they also knew that his involvement in the conspiracy was indirect. At least, that was what he hoped.

He realized how very naïve he had been to think that Ghani Ahmed was paying for his trip to participate in a religious camp. That had been a ruse—the real purpose of the trip was to have him trained in the use of explosives and weapons. Then why did they not do it, why didn't they train him to kill? He would've declined to participate. Would he? That was what he told everybody, but could he have been convinced? He was more confused now than he had been since his arrest. He tried to sleep but couldn't, and to kill time he prayed.

Next morning, while he was strolling in the yard, Eliot came to him carrying a pizza box.

"Hey Sand Nigger, meet my friend Jason," Eliot said.

"Hullo my friend," Jason greeted Rafiq. He was as tall as Eliot but muscular, and had deep blue eyes. Jason swiftly came towards Rafiq, and offered him his hand. To avoid him, Rafiq stepped aside, tripped and fell. Jason pinned him on the ground, and Eliot opened the pizza box. Rafiq saw the pink, round pepperoni slices on the pizza. He knew it was pork. He could smell it.

"Here, have some pizza," Eliot said, and tried to stuff the pizza into his mouth. Rafiq shut his mouth tight.

"Oh, don't you get it?" Jason said mockingly to Eliot. "He's a sand nigger, they don't eat pork. Here, give it to me." He grabbed the pizza slice from Eliot, then held Rafiq's neck in one hand, and pushed the pizza into his mouth with the other. Rafiq struggled to get away from him, but couldn't. He choked, trying to keep his mouth shut, tears streamed down his face. Jason was sitting on his chest, and Eliot was holding his legs.

Shawn came running over and pulled him up. Eric and Jason walked away, laughing. "What happened here?" the officer asked.

Rafiq was speechless. He turned around, and pointed a finger at Eliot and Jason, but found it impossible to speak; he was barely able to stand or breathe.

Shawn walked purposefully to Eliot and Jason. "Leave him alone.

He's just a kid. Get outta here right now," he shouted.

Jason was still holding the pizza in his hand, and as he passed Rafiq he leaned over and brushed it across his face. Rafiq wiped away the wetness. Shawn led him inside.

"Did they hurt you?" Shawn asked. Rafiq shook his head. Shawn sounded insincere. There was no concern on his face. "Why don't you come with me to the superintendent's office for a while?" Rafiq nodded. In the office, Shawn offered Rafiq a chair and sat beside him.

"Do you want some coffee?"

Rafiq shook his head again.

"Talk to me, treat me as your friend."

Rafiq looked at him blankly.

"I heard you got weapons training, and you learned to make IEDs," Shawn said, smiling. "We get weapons training, too, when we join the police. But I'm curious about IEDs—did you actually get to use them?"

"No, I didn't get any training. Look, I'm really tired. I want to sleep."

"Sure, we can talk later. I'll take you back to your cell and lock the door so they don't return to bother you."

So that was what this was all about. They wanted to know more, and because he hadn't answered their questions, they had used Shawn and the two thugs to intimidate him. Rafiq collapsed on the bed in exhaustion. When he came around, he found himself on the floor; he had passed urine in his prison clothes; his eyes were ablaze. He was thirsty and there was a dull pain in his back.

Fifteen

Ghani Ahmed had told Rafiq to prepare for a trip to Kathmandu to participate in a religious camp when they met at the restaurant in Mississauga. Rafiq wasn't sure he wanted to go that far to a strange country, but Ghani Ahmed persuaded him by telling him that this was his opportunity to meet young Muslims from all over North America and Europe to share experiences.

"You will meet jihadis from different parts of the world," he said.

"I guess I can take a few days off," Rafiq told him.

He had recently started working at Wanderlust, and lied to his employer Hameed that he was going to a workshop on philanthropy where he would be representing Nagma Khala's Thorncliffe Neighbourhood Centre. At home he lied to his family that Wanderlust was sending him to Nepal to attend a conference on e-commerce in the tourism industry.

Rafiq landed in Kathmandu in the late spring of 2007 with 300 American dollars in his wallet. Ghani Ahmed's instructions were simple. "Keep quiet, do what you are told, and drink only bottled water." At the airport, a man holding a signboard with his name took him in a taxi to a valley resort outside Lalitpur. Here he was to wait for further instructions.

The resort was swathed in lush green foliage amidst undulating Himalayan foothills. It was Rafiq's second trip outside Canada, the first being to Bombay with his mother and sister, and he was naturally a bit wary. He had never been to a tourist resort before, and he fell in love with beautiful Nepal. There was nobody at the resort at first—no teacher, no students, and no religious camp. Then a couple of days after his arrival, he received a phone call from a man who identified himself as "Ghani's friend" and instructed him to be ready to move to a hotel in Kathmandu.

He was taken by a different man to a cheap and rundown hotel in Thamel, a busy marketplace in Kathmandu clustered with shops and cafes. It was far more interesting than the resort. His room was booked for a week. With nothing to do for the first few days, Rafiq was bored and took long treks along the mountain trails outside the town.

After a couple of days, another man came to see him. They met in the hotel lounge. The visitor was dressed in a smart royal blue business jacket and chequered trousers. He was clean shaven and reeked of perfume. He shook hands with Rafiq and asked him to sit. He ordered "tea and toast" for them and smiled. Rafiq smiled in return and was on the point of asking him about the religious conference, when the man said, "There is a change of plan. You will be leaving for India early tomorrow morning."

"Where?"

"Ahmedabad. You will be meeting the victims of the 2002 riots."

Rafiq wasn't sure he wanted to make that trip but nodded. He was regretting his decision to come on this trip. He desperately wanted to talk to Ghani Ahmed and return home.

"When will I return to Toronto?"

"You will know when you are in Ahmedabad."

"I haven't even spoken to Ghani Ahmed."

"You can talk to him when you are in India."

The next morning, a taxi took him to the airport, and he boarded a Royal Nepal Airlines flight to Bombay, the city his parents still called home. The first thing that hit him with ferocious intensity when he landed in Bombay was the extreme heat and humidity. Spring in Canada occurred at the peak of summer in India. Within moments he was sweating profusely and gulping down prodigious quantities of bottled water.

Balu, a dapper man, transported him to a hotel close to the airport. It was obvious that Balu wasn't involved with Ghani Ahmed or his men, because he was quite at ease, knew nothing about Rafiq, and kept humming Hindi film songs. His car had photographs of multi-limbed Hindu gods and goddesses. In contrast, all the others he had met on the trip thus far had withheld their names from him, preferred to keep quiet, and seemed tense and edgy.

The hotel was at the end of a busy thoroughfare clogged with traffic and people. The car was supposedly air-conditioned but the equipment was faulty and Rafiq continued to sweat. Balu apologized and wended his way through the traffic to reach the hotel. A woman behind the reception desk checked him in, and Balu handed Rafiq a cellphone. Before walking back to his car, Balu told him to be ready at "five o'clock in the morning." He was to board an early morning train to Ahmedabad.

Rafiq dreaded the train journey because he knew it would be unbearably hot. Even inside the air-conditioned hotel room he felt uncomfortable. The room was stuffy and smelly. He remembered his earlier stay at another hotel during his last trip to Bombay, when he had been rather comfortable. He couldn't sleep until it was morning and time for him to leave. He tried calling Ghani Ahmed from the cellphone but gave up after a few unsuccessful attempts.

At dawn, he heard the azaan from a mosque. The muezzin's call to prayers was loud and clear. He found the rendition deeply moving. He hadn't heard anything so beautiful in Canada. He had a quick shower, performed the ritual ablution, and prayed. He wore light clothes, expecting a horrid time in the heat during the train journey. Balu drove him to a railway station called Borivali.

It was early morning but the heat was already severe. Balu stood in the queue, bought a ticket for him to Ahmedabad, and then accompanied him to the platform. An overpowering smell of shit enveloped the place, making Rafiq gag. The platform was a melange of the old and the new. Traditional travellers carried garish aluminum luggage boxes; the younger set carried smart-looking bags with wheels. All of them had a cellphone in their hands.

He was surprised by the sleek looks of the suburban trains and shocked to see the crowds even at this early hour. There were many food outlets on the platform. In the one nearest to them, a hot stew of potatoes and chickpeas was being cooked. His Abba and Ammi would have told him that it was the traditional Bombay usal, sufficiently tasty on its own, but a delectable delicacy when combined with the humble bread—called pao in the local Bambaiya dialect.

Chai was being brewed everywhere, its strong smell wafting across the platform. Balu ordered a cup of "cutting chai," and asked Rafiq if he wanted one too. Rafiq declined forcefully. The very idea of having food in the middle of all the squalor and filth was revolting. He was convinced he would die of diarrhea if he ate at the station.

Nearly every male was dressed in a shirt and trouser; a few wore the loose kurta, but nobody was in a dhoti, which was supposedly the traditional Indian attire. On the other hand almost all women wore Indian dresses—either a salwaar-kameez or a sari. A few younger women wore trousers and tops, and a few of them were in jeans. But unlike back home in Toronto, here the jeans weren't hip-hugging. There were a bunch of beggars—from very young children to infirm old men—hovering around the stinking toilets. They were probably waiting for the train to arrive to start begging. Stray dogs ran around the platform, looking for food or chasing one another or their own tails.

Balu had bought a ticket for the first class coach. A blue-coloured train arrived. It was on time and that surprised Rafiq because his parents always admired the punctual public transit of Canada, implying that this wasn't the norm in India. With Balu's help he located the first class coach and managed to step inside, a few minutes before the train pulled away. Balu waved him goodbye as the train left the platform.

Rafiq settled inside the coach. It was dank and dark, and had two parallel seats with an aisle in the middle, each of them for three passengers. Fifteen passengers were jostling for spaces. There was an overpowering smell of body odour. The fans were useless ancient contraptions whirring furiously but not circulating air. The train gathered speed, and hot wind blasted in from the windows, heating up the already warm compartment.

The passengers who were sitting lolled rhythmically to the train's movement, and within moments most of them dozed off. Rafiq found it hard to keep his balance. He kept drinking water and was sweating ceaselessly. After about fifteen minutes the train sped over a large body of water, when one of the passengers threw a marigold garland into it, folded his hands, closed his eyes, and bowed his head in prayers.

The train briefly stopped somewhere, and a group of hijras—transvestites or eunuchs—got into the coach, and loudly clapped and danced in the corridor outside the coupe. Rafiq was wonderstruck; he had read about hijras on the internet, but hadn't ever seen them. He remembered Ammi telling him that a group of hijras had danced at her wedding. The hijras zeroed in on Rafiq, and he couldn't help but smile at the leader of the group, a balding hijra with arched eyebrows and a painted face. When she asked him for money, Rafiq pulled out a five-hundred-rupee bill; she was ecstatic and her group members smiled, and cheered him as they walked away clacking and clapping.

Their loud and boisterous arrival had woken up many of the slumbering passengers. Some of them looked at Rafiq with a mixture of contempt and incomprehension, because he had paid the hijras.

"We will reach in about twenty minutes," a man said, addressing no one in particular.

The train came screeching to an agonizing halt. Everyone who was seated rushed out. Rafiq moved to the vacant window seat. The station had been newly redecorated, its building covered in ceramic tiles, and the platform walls freshly painted. A young man, carrying a wicker basket full of batata wada, spicy potato patties, and red, pungent chutney, was shouting into each window, calling out his ware. There were many takers. A boy wearing only shorts came inside the coach, carrying a kettle full of piping hot chai.

As the train moved out of the station, Rafiq felt the hot air hit him and singe his face. His back was hurting. He was tired and wanted to return home. There was now just one other passenger in the compartment. The other passenger bought two cups of chai from the vendor and gave one to Rafiq.

"This will be relaxing," he said with finality. Rafiq took the cup and sipped the chai; it was refreshing. The man looked at Rafiq with interest, and asked, "You are an NRI, right?" Rafiq didn't know what that meant and said so.

"Non-Resident Indian, actually they should be called Not Required Indians," the man said and laughed.

"I'm Canadian," Rafiq replied, affably.

"You look like an Indian."

"No, I mean, I'm a Canadian citizen."

"Canada . . . it is a cold place, I hear."

"Yes."

The man smiled, apparently happy that long winters were an immense inconvenience for a person from the tropics, howsoever long he may have been in Canada.

"You should be careful with food, you know," the man said with concern. "You people can't digest Indian foods and drinks."

"It's too late. I've already had tea . . . chai," Rafiq said, in mock anxiety.

"Don't worry. The worst that can happen is a minor bout of Delhi belly." He winked at Rafiq.

The view from the window was of a surreal painting, the green of the trees mixed with the grey of the clouds, melting into each other. Rafiq shut his eyes to avoid further conversation.

—⁓—

Rafiq reached Ahmedabad late in the afternoon. He stepped down from the train and called the number Balu had given him. A woman answered and told him to walk out of the station to the main concourse. There a woman wearing a white salwaar-kameez walked up to him. She was about his Ammi's age, dark-skinned, and wore thin-rimmed glasses. Her head was uncovered. She greeted him and took him to a waiting car, which had working air-conditioning. Rafiq sighed with relief. There were more people here than he had seen at Borivali station in Bombay. Ramshackle buses exhaled noxious black fumes as they heaved angrily out of the terminal. There were a few ox-carts too.

"I'm Razia. I'm the secretary of the 2002 Gujarat Riot Victims Welfare Forum; it is an NGO to create awareness of the continuing plight of the victims," the woman said. Rafiq nodded. He was tired after the hot and exhausting journey.

"Are you hungry?" Razia asked. Rafiq shook his head. He just wanted to get out of this place. It took them forever to reach the hotel, though the distance they travelled wasn't long. Before driving off, Razia told him that she would pick him up in the morning to take him to visit some of the families who had lost everything during the riots. Rafiq went to his room. He had a shower, but the water was hard and the shampoo wouldn't foam enough. He came out and called Ghani Ahmed. He finally got through and couldn't stop protesting.

"I've no idea why I'm here. I've done absolutely nothing so far, but gone from one place to another."

"Rafiq, it is not safe to talk on the phone. The Ahmedabad group doesn't know me. Go and meet some of the families; it will help you to understand their plight. It will give you a perspective. This is how Muslims suffer in the world."

Rafiq wanted to complain more and tell his mentor that he knew perfectly well what it meant to be a victim of a riot because he was one himself, but Ghani Ahmed hung up. Rafiq ordered a tandoori chicken and a can of Coke but wasn't able to eat, and began to shiver. By the time it was dark outside he was unable to keep still, and called the hotel staff for help. A steward knocked on the door, put his hand to Rafiq's face and gave him a pill. He fell asleep immediately. He woke up to loud banging on the door. The steward informed him that Razia was waiting for him in the lobby. He was not at all interested in going out in the heat but had no choice, so he slowly changed into fresh clothes and went down. Razia couldn't hide her disapproval.

"I have fever."

"Do you want to come with us?" Razia said.

"I may have to return."

They drove to what Razia said was the "old, walled city," and Rafiq immediately noticed that this part of the city was more rundown. They reached the welfare centre, and Rafiq followed Razia inside. A few women, some wearing a burka and others with their heads covered with dupattas, were sitting on the floor. At Razia's prodding, one after another they narrated their stories. Most of them spoke in Gujarati, some in Hindustani. Razia translated into English. Rafiq was shocked by the stories. He had heard of the violence and the rioting, how vicious they had been, but he could never have imagined the horrors these people, especially women, lived through. Reliving their tragedy with them disturbed him, and he began to cry, his tears flowing freely and abundantly. He fainted.

Razia ended the meeting and helped Rafiq get into the car. She told the driver to take them to a hospital. She seemed to know everyone at the hospital, and after a brief wait Rafiq was taken to a private ward where he was administered saline. A woman doctor came and checked his pulse; she asked him routine questions, and then declared to Razia, "He has had sunstroke. He is dehydrated. Nothing serious." She advised him to rest for a couple of days. He spent those days at the hospital doing nothing except watching television.

On the day of his departure, Razia took him to the airport.

"Who do you arrange these visits for?" he asked her.

"For anyone who is willing to listen to these people and help them," Razia replied.

"Do you know Ghani Ahmed?" Rafiq asked, even though his mentor had said Razia's group didn't know him, and had specifically instructed him not to talk about him and his work.

"No. Where is he from? London?"

"Toronto . . . Tell me, what's the solution to such hatred?" he asked, hurriedly changing the subject. "How can you put up with it?"

"Definitely not by hating back." There was a curious but amused look on her face.

"Should Muslims just keep quiet, then? Do nothing?"

"What can they do?"

"Retaliate in revenge?"

"How can that be a solution? It would only aggravate the situation."

Rafiq wanted to talk more but remembered Ghani Ahmed's instruction and said no more. He boarded a flight to Delhi and then from there, another flight brought him back to Toronto.

Sixteen

After his frightening encounter with Eliot and Jason, Rafiq was rest-less and wary. He expected more harassment, and though Shawn kept a watchful eye on him, and his tormentors stayed away, he couldn't help feeling that they were all together. It seemed rather obvious to him: Eliot and Jason had intimidated him, and Shawn had magically come to his rescue, only to gain his confidence. They wanted to know about his trip, and his supposed weapons training.

He almost wished he had something to tell them. Rafiq was cer-tain that the CSIS officers who had questioned him knew the facts, and would have known that his involvement with Ghani Ahmed was peripheral at best. He had learned more about his trip talking to them than from Ghani Ahmed. He was both surprised and intrigued that the cops believed him to be a hardboiled Islamic terrorist.

"Believe me, nothing happened. Nothing at all," Rafiq told Shawn, on more than one occasion, and each time, Shawn smiled knowingly. He didn't want to believe Rafiq because for him that was too simple an answer. There had to be more.

To keep his mind off his grim situation, Rafiq prayed and read from the Quran often, and reminisced about his days in school. He often thought of Sufiya Quadri. She joined Middle School when Rafiq was in his last year there. He was a gawky and gaunt teenager, having just returned from Bombay, where he witnessed the romance between his sister and his cousin. His world consisted of home, school, and Nagma Khala's crèche, where he helped her look after the younger kids, and also monopolized the computer. Sufiya had large round grey eyes with a hint of mischief in them, and mile-long eyelashes. Her small nose sat delicately on her square face, and her chin was sturdy. She covered her head in a hijab, and wore a cape and a long dress. He had seen only her face and hands. He couldn't help feeling that Sufiya was a girl who had been forced to become a woman much too soon.

Sufiya had immigrated to Toronto with her parents from India, from a small town near Surat called Khim, north of Bombay. An only child, she was older than him, and should have been in Grade 9, but the school authorities had placed her in Grade 8 because they concluded her English language skills wouldn't be adequate. Rafiq thought that was an absurd decision because while Sufiya no doubt had a thick accent, she knew the language better than most others in the classroom.

She was ready with an answer to every question. Her stolen glances gave him reasons to believe that she liked him. But when he tried to speak to her, she would walk away without answering, or merely say yes or no. After days of rehearsing before the washroom mirror at home, he finally gathered enough courage to walk confidently up to her in school. She was standing by the water fountain. He tried to smile but couldn't. All his rehearsing and all his courage had simply evaporated in her presence. She smiled ever so slightly to avoid the embarrassment and the awkwardness of the situation. Then she turned to return to the classroom.

"Sufiya, wait . . . " he called and ran to catch up with her. She stopped and looked at him, a rolled-up notebook in one hand.

Rafiq grabbed her hand, but she pulled it back.

"No. Don't touch me. What is it, Rafiq?"

Again, he couldn't speak.

That evening, when Rafiq reached Nagma Khala's crèche to help her, she asked him why he was quiet. She was wrapping meals and putting them in paper bags for the community centre to distribute among poor immigrant families. Looking at his long face, she knew something was bothering him. She called Ruksana, but she wasn't home. Ziram answered the phone.

"I hope he is not being bullied at school," Nagma said.

"He probably just doesn't want to do his homework."

But when he got home, Ziram, too, realized something indeed was wrong with her weird brother.

"Have you been crying? What's going on?"

Rafiq looked at her, went into the bedroom, and slammed the door shut. Ziram refocused her attention on the latest Hindi movie. Rafiq couldn't stay alone for long, and returned to the living room. Agitated, he went to the kitchen looking for some snack, randomly banging cupboard doors. She ignored him.

"I'm hungry, and there is nothing to eat. When is Ammi back?" he demanded.

"Not till midnight. She's doing the evening shift. What's with you?"

Rafiq shuffled his feet, curled and uncurled his toes, looked at the TV, and then at his sister.

"There's this new girl in school . . . Sufiya," he said in a soft and tenuous voice.

"Who? Speak up."

"Sufiya."

"Oh, that girl from India. I know her. She is quite cute. Short and plump but cute," Ziram said.

Rafiq smiled shyly.

"I see her at the bus stop. Her house is just behind ours. What about her?"

"I think I love her," he mumbled.

Ziram laughed derisively, but then said, "She's just your type, isn't she?"

"Huh?"

"She's the mullah-type. Covering her head and wearing a whole lot of unnecessary clothes. Tell her about Nagma Khala, and how you waste your time there on prayers and stuff. I'm sure she'll be interested."

"But I can't say a word to her."

"I'll tell her when I meet her next."

"No, you won't."

"Suit yourself."

When Abdul returned home, Ziram had to switch off the TV. Rafiq changed into his jeans, and put on his light blue hoodie. "I'm going to Nagma Khala's place," he announced. At the crèche, Nagma was busy with the kids and their parents: it was pickup time. When everyone had left, she asked him to join her in offering the evening namaaz. Show me the right path, he said in his mind, praying alongside Nagma Khala.

"What is the matter?" she asked. "You look sad."

Rafiq hesitated. "I love a girl, and I don't know how to tell her." He told her about Sufiya. Nagma Khala listened to him, and then kept quiet for a long time.

"Say something, Khala."

"You may think you have grown up but, Beta, you are still too young to think about all this. You have a long road ahead of you; study hard, get a job, buy a house, support your parents, and make their lives better, more comfortable. That should take another fifteen years. Think about marrying when you are man, not when you are a boy."

"You just don't get it, do you?" he said, unable to hide his dismay. "Where does marriage come into this?"

"You listen to me now. We are Muslims and we are not white people. Marriages are decided by elders. And don't talk about this to anyone because you will spoil that girl's life forever."

Rafiq had thought that Nagma Khala understood him, but he was totally mistaken. For the first time, she had raised her voice talking to him. He felt bothered that first Ziram had ridiculed him and now Nagma Khala had got mad with him. He had to talk to Ammi. After Abba went to the bedroom, and Ammi was doing the dishes, he told her about Sufiya. Ruksana looked at him in surprise. Her initial reaction was predictable. "Aren't you very young for this sort of thing?" she asked. But when she saw his face, she smiled and asked him: "You have a photo of the girl?"

"No. Ammi, that girl doesn't talk to me."

"Have you told your father?"

"Are you crazy?"

"Ziram?"

"Yes, she laughed at me, and I also told Nagma Khala, and she got mad at me."

"Nagma belongs to the seventeenth century. What does she know about love? She only knows to pray and to cook."

"That's so unfair, Ammi."

"You will leap to her defence, won't you?"

"Ammi, what should I do?"

"Be patient. Be decent. Be nice. Don't do anything that would create problems either for you or for her."

Rafiq wasn't entirely satisfied, but he was reassured. At least Ammi hadn't lectured him as Nagma Khala had.

—⁘—

Sufiya's family lived in the basement of a house near the school. When Rafiq learned this, he gave up the school bus. His parents were surprised. Rafiq had always preferred to take the bus, because he hated the cold weather.

"Is someone bullying you on the bus?" Ruksana asked.

"No, Ammi."

Rafiq would leave home early and wait at the intersection near the school for Sufiya to come by. She walked fast and purposefully. He would follow her at some distance. After a few days of this, an annoyed Sufiya asked him in her thick accent, "Why are you following me?"

Rafiq had rehearsed his answers, but he just gaped at her beautiful frowning face.

"You idiot, are you going to say something?" she shouted.

"I'm not going to take the school bus anymore."

"But why are you following me?"

Rafiq said nothing. She meaningfully tapped her forehead—indicating he was crazy—and walked away. He followed a few steps behind her. She stopped, turned, and shouted, "Will you just stop that! You either walk with me or walk on the other side of the road. Don't follow me."

He lumbered up to her. Success at last, he thought, but still he had no idea what to say to her. When they reached the school, he asked her, "Can I walk back home with you after school?"

She shrugged. "If you want to. At least that way you won't follow me."

He was ecstatic. He wanted to tell the world that he was in love.

Walking together every day, he saw her in new ways. She was taller than him but had a child's feet. Her hands were dainty, and she had the long fingers of an artist. Of course, he hadn't known that artists had long fingers until, she explained, grinning broadly, that she could draw and paint well because she had "artist's fingers."

She told him that her parents had been civil engineers in India. He had no idea what civil engineers did. Here they held survival jobs. Her mother worked at the local Canadian Tire, and her father at Wal-Mart. She had many relatives and friends. Her dad would soon start taking courses to get another degree, and her mother planned to do the same after he completed his program.

Rafiq wanted her to try tobogganing. He had to explain what that meant. He liked the sport because he could do it all by himself, it didn't need a team or even another player. Climb slowly up the cliff, while pulling the toboggan behind you, reach the top and survey the snow-covered landscape beneath your feet. In a state of elation he would sit on the toboggan and push himself downhill, starting slowly and then gathering speed up to a heart-stopping velocity as he hurtled down before coming to rest in a shower of snow at the bottom. From his description, Sufiya agreed that it was thrilling.

"It sounds like fun but let me see you do it."

She promised to come the next Saturday afternoon to the community park. Rafiq didn't expect her to come but she did. He went down the snowy hill a few times to demonstrate, and then he insisted she do it, too. Sufiya was hesitant, but he helped her climb the slope, holding her hand and pulling her. She sat gingerly on the toboggan and held on to dear life as it plummeted down the slope; near the bottom it swerved and threw her off. Rafiq ran down. He pulled her up, and she held him tight.

As though they had suddenly grown up, they moved apart. Her hijab had slid off her head, and her hair fell across her face; she didn't stop him when he brushed it back, but her face turned crimson. She was beautiful!

"Do you want to do it again?"

"Yes!"

It was dark when they returned home. At the door she turned around and asked him to come in and meet her parents.

Rafiq was uncertain. "What'll I do, meeting them?"

"Nothing. Just talk to them."

Her parents were cooking. That was the first difference he saw between her family and his. For Abba cooking was something he had to do in this new country because it was expected of men to share in household chores. Sufiya's father seemed to enjoy cooking. He shook hands with Rafiq. "I'm Ismail and this is Saleema." He wore a loose white shirt that reached down to his knees and a white pyjama that was way too short. His beard and hair were coloured red, dyed in henna. Saleema was wearing a plain yellow salwaar-kameez, and looked like an older version of Sufiya.

Rafiq was, as usual in such circumstances, tongue-tied, and Sufiya declared, "He is very shy."

"I'm not!"

Everyone laughed.

They invited him to dinner. Sufiya's dad led Rafiq to a small wash-basin to wash his hands, and Sufiya helped her mother bring the food. They sat on the floor in the living room on a piece of cloth that Sufiya's dad called a dastarkhan; it was a special carpet for sitting to have food. Rafiq waited for Sufiya and her mother to join them but realized that they wouldn't when her dad said, "Bismillah—In the name of God."

Sufiya didn't remove her headscarf and cape at home. Rafiq found this strange. He knew they were devout Muslims, but what he didn't understand was why she had taken him home, and why her parents had seemed so casual about it.

He got home late. When Ruksana called him for dinner, Rafiq didn't want to eat.

"What did Nagma cook today?"

"I ate at Sufiya's place."

Abdul and Ruksana exchanged a surprised look, Ruksana giving the briefest smile, but they both remained quiet. When Ziram came to the table and saw Rafiq on the couch, she demanded, "Why's he not having dinner?"

"He has had dinner at his in-laws' home," Ruksana said. Abdul chortled.

Rafiq smiled too. After Abdul went to bed, Ruksana asked, "What was dinner like?"

"Ammi, you know, Sufiya and her mother didn't eat with us."

"Feudal!"

—⁘—

It was a few weeks before Rafiq asked Sufiya about that evening. She said her parents had allowed her to go tobogganing only if she would then bring Rafiq home. They had wanted to be sure she was going out with a friend.

"And what did they say after they met me?"

"They said you are a good friend."

"But I'm more than a friend."

They were a few steps from the intersection where they would go their different ways. She held his hand tight and said, "We can only be friends."

Rafiq tried to smile but couldn't. Slowly they parted and took their different roads. He was feeling desolate.

The sidewalk had been mostly cleared of snow. A plastic chocolate-bar wrapper fluttered forlornly in the wind. Oblivious of the cold, which he usually hated, Rafiq wondered why Sufiya was rejecting him. Surely, their one-year age difference shouldn't matter. There had to be another reason. Perhaps there was someone else. Perhaps she was already engaged: Ammi had told him that when she was growing up in India some girls were married when they were kids. Maybe Sufiya was married.

It couldn't be true that he was nothing more than a friend to her.

They continued to walk to and from school and to go tobogganing on Saturdays. They studied together. If Rafiq was willing to forget that he loved this pretty girl, everything was fine. She was, indeed, a good friend.

Sufiya came home to meet Ziram and his parents. She seemed adept at managing awkward situations and handled the flow of conversation with ease. Ammi was happy that he was spending less time at Nagma's place, and Abba was relieved that he was, after all, a normal boy.

When it was time to choose a high school, Rafiq wanted to go to the same school as Sufiya, and take the same subjects, but Abba insisted he attend a school that had a program in computer science.

As usual, Sufiya was wise beyond her years.

"You must do what will help you succeed. I'm doing that."

She would go to a different school. Rafiq sensed dejection in her voice, he was sure he wasn't imagining it. "Are you sure?" he asked. They were walking back from school the day before the summer break.

"Yes, I'm sure."

—∞—

Time passed. In the summer between Grades 9 and 10, Sufiya's family went to India for a wedding and didn't return. Ismail had found a job in his profession in Abu Dhabi.

Rafiq never saw Sufiya again. They exchanged emails for some time, but the frequency declined until finally they stopped communicating completely. When they rediscovered each other on Facebook some years later, their lives had changed. From her profile he learnt that she was married to a Memon Gujarati engineer and settled in Abu Dhabi. Rafiq was involved with Ghani Ahmed. But every time he saw her photograph on Facebook, he remembered their happy times together with a twinge of melancholy in his heart.

IV

Home Again

Seventeen

Rafiq hoped the CSIS officers would return to ask him more questions. The first time they came he was scared and unsure. Now he knew what he wanted to say. He would tell them that he regretted his involvement with Ghani Ahmed, and that he was certain the mastermind of the conspiracy had dropped him. In the loneliness of the prison cell, he asked himself uncomfortable questions, which he had swept under the carpet before. He had been naïve and careless. Unthinking, in the shelter of his home, in his life with his family.

He didn't believe in Ghani Ahmed's program of violence, but had Ghani Ahmed actually dropped him from his group? He wanted to believe that, but then why did he ask Rafiq to go to Nepal and India, and why did Rafiq go? What did he expect? He was not sure. It was less the lure of travel and more wanting to share experiences with others of his kind, meeting other young Muslims who might feel like him. Here in Canada there was no one he could talk to about his faith, especially someone of his own age.

But was the trip's actual purpose that or was it to train him to use weapons and become a genuine terrorist? He had not seen a weapon during that trip. He had not seen a weapon in his life except in movies. There also was the question, who were the other members of Ghani Ahmed's group? He had not thought about these issues. Perhaps he did not want to think about them. His Abba would have said, "It is one thing to lie to the world, and quite another to lie to yourself."

He wondered why the interrogators hadn't asked him anything specifically about Ghani Ahmed, and why they had asked him about mundane things such as how his family had lived in Canada from the time they immigrated, what were their monthly expenses, how he got his job at Wanderlust, and how Abba got his job at Sloan Auto.

Enforced and prolonged solitude inside his cell gave him time to consider everything that had happened to him with a certain detachment, and the more he thought about his involvement with Ghani Ahmed the more he realized how stupid he had been, and how diabolical Ghani Ahmed was. Was this what it meant to be young?—to be naïve and foolish and yet cocky?

He was angry with himself; he just couldn't come to terms with what he saw as his betrayal of his parents. He knew his father would never forgive him for embracing Ghani Ahmed's worldview. His conflict with his dad wasn't about money. His family had been poor ever since he remembered—in Canada and in India—and they knew how to live with little.

Their conflict was about belief. He began to realize that he had been misguided, and if he had mustered enough courage to discuss his views with Abba, he wouldn't be in prison now. He still couldn't completely agree with his father's views. Abba claimed to be a liberal ("do your duties before claiming your rights") but was often intolerant of any views other than his own. Ammi supported Rafiq because she was his mother and loved him, not because she believed in his cause.

He had failed everyone. Ammi and Abba had made a lifetime of sacrifices, done a lifetime of hard work; they had forfeited their hopes and dreams so that their children could succeed. Ironically, both Abdul and Ruksana continued to struggle and fight their circumstances, despite repeated failures, so that their kids wouldn't have to support them. Ziram had struggled, too, to overcome her own tragedy. He, Rafiq, was the only one in the family who hadn't had to sacrifice, and what had he given them in return? Misery and despondency.

Abba's recent layoff, and now Rafiq's own ignominious arrest, had brought them back to ground zero. The court case would cost a lot; if the case dragged on for long, they would have to sell their dream house, their destiny. What a destiny! Abba had said they could seek legal aid if necessary, but Rafiq wasn't sure that was possible since he had been charged under the anti-terrorism law. And if, after all that, he lost his case, how many years would he have to spend in jail? What would become of him? He had already had a taste of the horrors of prison life.

There would be no sympathy for him, a Muslim believed to be a terrorist; it would affect him for a long time.

He had always been a failure. He hadn't done anything of any consequence and now he would in all likelihood spend the rest of his life in prison. What difference would that make to anyone? Would it even matter whether he lived or died? He didn't have to live because nobody would miss him if he died. Of course, they wouldn't tell him that to his face, but surely if he died, they would be relieved rather than aggrieved. The more he thought about his death, the more the idea appealed to him.

He thought of ways in which he could end his life. He could strangle himself with the bed sheet, as he had heard it done in movies; he didn't know exactly how, and the cell didn't have anything to hang it from. He could sneak a kitchen knife from the prison cafeteria, but that didn't seem possible or easy. There was no way to reach the roof of the building to jump to his death. He could ask one of the other inmates—perhaps Eric or Jason—to strangle him, but that was too far-fetched. Why would they or anyone else agree? The detention centre was suicide-proof.

Later that evening an officer took him to meet Anita. She said she had come just to tell him that she planned to move the bail plea, and that he should be ready.

"Will my parents be there?"

"Yes, of course."

"CSIS officers interrogated me a couple of days back."

She didn't seem surprised to hear this. "What did they ask?"

"Nothing about Ghani Ahmed, nothing about the plan. Random questions about my past."

She nodded.

"Two other prisoners tried to force me to eat pork and an officer then asked me about my trip to Nepal. He was sympathetic, but I think he is part of a plan with those two prisoners and CSIS. They are trying to get more information from me."

"Did they beat you?"

"Yes. I think it was more a ploy to get me to speak up. I wish I could tell them more. Unfortunately, there's really nothing to tell."

"Your parents told me that when they came to meet you an officer kept them locked inside a room for a long time, and another one asked questions about you and Ghani Ahmed," Anita said.

"The officer who helped me is Shawn," Rafiq said.

"That's the guy. He spoke to your parents."

"What does all this mean?" Rafiq asked. He was scared.

"I'll talk to the superintendent. This shouldn't happen. I'll make sure it doesn't happen again," Anita said.

"What about the bail?"

"Yes, we're moving your bail, so just hang in there for a little while longer. We're going to need the Asian community's support. I've talked to your parents. Your dad will talk to your neighbour to get a support letter from the Milton Gurdwara, but he said he's not sure if that'll come through. Jameel said he'll try to get a letter from Sheridan College, some sort of a character reference."

"Talk to Nagma Khala. She'll be able to get letters from her community centre in Thorncliffe Park. I did a lot of voluntary work for it. She may even convince other Muslim community leaders to lend support."

"Yes, that's a good suggestion. We need as much support as we can get."

"Talk to Ziram. She'll talk to Nagma Khala," Rafiq said.

—�—

On her way out, Anita requested for a meeting with the Superintendent of the detention centre. Kenneth Peterson, the Superintendent, agreed to meet her after making her wait for some time. He had a large, well-appointed office. His work desk was cluttered with paper and office stationery. He got up from his chair and walked over to greet Anita. Peterson was a big man. The colour of his eyes matched his short steel grey hair. His nose sat like a small red bulb on his face, and his mouth opened wide when he smiled. He led Anita to a couch at the other end of his office.

"Good afternoon Ms Persaud. How may I help you today?" he asked.

"I've come to talk to you about Rafiq Latif. He's an inmate here, kept in isolation . . . "

"For his own safety," Peterson interrupted.

"Yet he's being harassed and tortured," Anita said.

"You realize that it is a grave charge, Ms Persaud," Peterson said.

"My client has informed me that one of your officers, Shawn, has been deliberately looking away while some inmates intimidate him."

"On the contrary, Ms Persaud, my information is that Shawn has actually tried to help your client. I've been told that some inmates misbehaved with this young man on a couple of occasions, and on both occasions our officer intervened, and prevented anything untoward."

"So you admit that my client was manhandled?"

"I'm admitting to no such thing. Our officer prevented it twice."

"Shawn also locked up my client's parents when they had come here to meet him," Anita said.

"That is not true. He actually opened the door to the room and let them out. Another officer had mistakenly taken them to the room," Peterson said.

Anita realized that Peterson had been thoroughly briefed. He wasn't going to admit to any misdemeanour on the part of his officers. She had to change her approach.

"Mr Peterson, if this harassment doesn't stop, I'll talk to the media about what's going on inside Maplehurst. I'm sure the *Toronto Star* will be very interested to know all the sordid details."

This unsettled Peterson, and Anita detected a hint of panic in his eyes. His tone changed from officious to conciliatory.

"Ms Persaud, I assure you that nothing wrong has happened in my detention centre, and I assure you that I'll talk to my officers to ensure that nothing wrong does ever happen here. We run this place professionally."

"I'll also talk to the ethnic South Asian media . . . "

"I said I'll look into this. Now, is there anything else I can do for you, Ms Persaud? I have a hectic schedule ahead of me, so, if you'll excuse me, I've gotta return to my work." He got up from the couch and shook Anita's hand. He led her to the door, opened it for her and shook her hand again. "Thank you and have a nice day."

—◊◊◊—

A couple of days later, a team of officers drove Rafiq to the courthouse and brought him into the courtroom through a side door. Abba, Ammi, Ziram, Jameel, and Kartar were present. They smiled uncertainly when they saw him and he tried to smile back. Facing them was the judge— a middle-aged man who managed the impossible feat of looking both alert and bored simultaneously. Rafiq couldn't make much of the interchange between the judge, the Crown Attorney, Anita, and the court officials. It seemed to be all about paperwork and nothing about him.

When the hearing began, Anita called on Kartar, who was putting up the bail money, to testify. He said he had known the family for a long time and they were respected members of the South Asian community. Abba, looking nervous and sad, pledged Rafiq's presence at home till the court case concluded. The family had managed to get support pledges from many sources. Nagma had obtained letters from the Thorncliffe Park centre, and also from a local mosque, a Muslim women's centre, the local Liberal Party leader, and prominent Muslim small entrepreneurs.

Of course, the Crown Attorney argued that Rafiq shouldn't be granted bail, calling him a hard-nosed terrorist and danger to society. He didn't sound convincing. Anita also informed the court that Rafiq had been manhandled inside the detention centre, and that prolonging his incarceration could lead to more such incidents. She assured the court that her client would be available for interrogation whenever required.

The bail was granted and set at $200,000. The date of the trial was to be determined later. Rafiq was to have no contact with Ghani Ahmed or any of his associates. He would have no access to computers or telephones. His passport would have to be deposited. He would have to wear an ankle bracelet to monitor his movements, which would be restricted.

With these restrictions imposed on his freedom, Rafiq was now free to go home. Abba and Ammi hugged him, as did Ziram, and Jameel showed his pleasure with a smile, though Rafiq couldn't help noticing that his sister and her husband exchanged nervous glances at Ammi's uncontained joy.

"This is just bail, the case goes on," Anita cautioned them. "It doesn't mean he has been acquitted of the charges."

Ziram and Jameel left for work and Kartar for his shop. Anita returned to her office in Toronto. Ruksana told Ziram to inform Nagma about Rafiq's bail. As Abdul drove Rafiq and Ruksana home, Rafiq's eyes remained riveted on the road and the traffic; he relished his freedom, however precarious; he couldn't believe he was out, that everything around him was real, that he was not in a dream.

But he wasn't able to relax. After what he had gone through in the detention centre, relaxation was impossible, and he wasn't sure he wanted to talk about his experiences to his parents. Suddenly, uncontrollably, he began to cry; tears ran down his face. He was sitting in front beside Abba, so fortunately Ammi didn't notice. Abba glanced nervously at him. "Are you all right?" He was a cautious driver and didn't like to talk while driving.

"What is wrong?" Ruksana asked anxiously from the back seat.

"I couldn't sleep, because the lights are always on there. You know I can't sleep with lights on," he mumbled.

"Did something happen?" Abdul asked again.

Rafiq was quiet. He wasn't sure whether he should tell his parents about his humiliation in prison.

"Did they torture you?" Ruksana asked anxiously.

"Two officers asked me all kinds of questions," he said.

"Well, yes we know you were interrogated. That was only to be expected," Abdul said.

"It wasn't just that. Two inmates . . . " Rafiq said, and sobbed again. "'They beat me up," he said, between sobs. "They forced me to eat pork."

"When did this happen? Why didn't you tell us about it until now?"

Abdul asked. His voice shook, having risen to a high pitch. Ruksana began to cry.

"I told Anita."

Ruksana calmed herself and said, "Anita knows what she is doing. Saabji, focus on the road."

At home, Abdul wanted to ask Rafiq about the interrogation but feared he might aggravate his son's discomfort. He was convinced that Rafiq had been tortured and wanted to ask Anita what they should do about it. He didn't want it to be covered up. If they were imposing restrictions on his son, he wanted them to be made accountable for what they had done to him inside the detention centre. They sat in silence. Rafiq knew his parents were expecting him to talk but he didn't know what more to talk about. He got up from the couch and walked to the window.

It was still early and he had absolutely no idea what to do for the rest of the day. Although he knew he wasn't supposed to use his cellphone, he wanted to call Ghani Ahmed just to tell him that he had suffered because of him. But his parents would misunderstand and he was sure the police would get to know of it, and he'd get into trouble. He wanted to take a walk, probably go to the Westwood Mall but wasn't sure he was allowed to do that.

"Rafiq." Abdul spoke up, unable to keep quiet any longer. "If they tortured you, we should speak to Anita about it, we shouldn't keep quiet."

"I told you what happened, and I told Anita what happened, too, I don't want to talk about it," Rafiq said in a low voice.

"Beta, there may be legal issues involved," Abdul said.

"Abba, Anita informed the court."

Rafiq was alarmed that his parents were getting so worked up about the incident. Anita had emphatically talked about it in the court, but both Abba and Ammi had been too nervous there to understand what was going on. He saw the anxiety on their faces, though they were doing their best to seem and sound normal. He switched on the TV. The newscaster announced the death of Debbie, the oldest polar bear in Canada, and then spoke of a murder in downtown Toronto.

Abdul looked at the TV and said, "Last week there was an explosion in BC at a gas pipeline. But it was an accident."

Rafiq didn't know what to do or say. He wasn't sure what Abba was implying, what was on his mind. His homecoming was turning out to be uncomfortable for them all. He went down to the basement but didn't find his laptop. He went to the upstairs study. The smell of cleaning fluid was overpowering. He had always thought that his Ammi's obsession with mopping the floors was inexplicable. The desktop computer was missing. He ran downstairs.

"Where are all my computers?"

"Don't you remember, the police took them and your cellphone," Abdul said.

"Didn't they return . . . ? Did they say when they'll return them?"

"No. I think they want them as evidence."

He remembered that the bail order had specified that he was not to use the computers, but he hadn't realized that he would literally have no access. He knew it was wiser not to go anywhere near a computer. Having learned from his parents that one of Ghani Ahmed's associates had called them, he was sure Ghani Ahmed would have sent him an email. That thought disturbed him. Why did his people call them, why would he send him an email, why after not communicating for more than a year? Would he do that to punish him, or misdirect the police? He was certain the police were already monitoring all his emails and phone calls. He decided to take a risk and visit the internet café at the mall. He changed into a fresh t-shirt and trousers and asked his mother for twenty dollars. He told her he wished to taste his freedom, go to the mall and look around. When he stepped outside, it was windy. He returned to grab his hoodie.

When he reached the Malton bus station, he abruptly changed his mind and took a bus to go to Nagma Khala's place. There were no other passengers in the overheated bus. The driver, looking smart in her uniform, greeted him with a nod. He wished he had taken the car. The bus filled up, mostly with noisy South Asian passengers. After a long and leisurely drive, the bus arrived on Lawrence Avenue West, the road on which the family had lived for eleven years in an apartment.

The route revived old memories: going to school, strolling home with Sufiya, the long solitary walks when he had become convinced that he had a special mission in life—to work with Ghani Ahmed for Muslims everywhere, in the name of Allah. He was committed now, too, but his commitment had to be through a different path—the path of service; Nagma Khala's path, not Ghani Ahmed's path.

Nagma Khala was surprised to see him. She blessed him the traditional way, touching his head with both her hands, cupping her palms into fists and softly touching her fingers to the side of her head and cracking her knuckles. It was the ritual for exorcising the evil eye, or seeking heavenly intervention to bring good luck. It amused him every time she performed the ritual. Although it was late, some kids were still around; that wasn't unusual, because many parents worked in shifts, their kids spending up to twelve hours at Nagma's crèche.

She went to the kitchen and got a bowl of sugar; she gave some to him and had a pinch herself. "Not good for my diabetes," she said and hugged him lightly where he stood. Rafiq was surprised, Nagma Khala had just broken her own strict rule of not touching the kids under her care, and she wouldn't let them touch each other either. She sat down on the floor mattress and motioned for him to do the same, beside her. The kids looked puzzled—they had always seen her smile but seldom seen her happy. One of them finally picked up courage to ask, "Is he your son?"

"Yes, he is my Beta, just as all of you are."

"No, I mean real son."

"Yes, real son," Nagma Khala said, and laughed, and tears rolled down her face.

"Why're you crying?" the kid asked.

"Am I? I didn't realize," Nagma replied and hastily wiped her face with her dupatta. "Now play."

The kids returned to their merry-making. Nagma Khala looked at Rafiq, tears flowing down her cheeks again. He didn't have to say anything. He wouldn't have known what to say. Soon the mothers arrived to pick up their kids. When the last one was gone, Nagma Khala asked him: "What was it like in prison?"

Rafiq didn't respond immediately, but then said, "I prayed and read from the Quran whenever I was depressed." He spoke softly, sounding uncertain. He didn't want to share his humiliating experience with her.

"I think your parents blame me for all this."

"What do you mean?"

"They must think that you have turned religious because of my influence."

"But Ammi is religious, too."

"Your father's silly notions have dented her belief, I think," Nagma said.

"I don't know. Sometimes I don't think he is against religion, but then at other times, I'm not sure. But they blame Ghani Ahmed, not you."

"And I think they are right."

"Khala, I don't know. I mean, I agree that killing innocent people is wrong, but I still don't think seeking justice is wrong."

"Yes, seeking justice isn't wrong. But what is justice?"

"I don't know why I stayed with Ghani Ahmed even after I disagreed with his methods."

"To defy your father. You rebelled against your Abba because he tried so hard to fit into this society, which ignored his Muslim identity, and you couldn't come to terms with him willing to lose his dignity."

Nagma Khala brought a big bowl of curried chickpeas and a bowl of rice from the kitchen.

"Have you thought about what you will do now?" she asked.

"I don't know."

"You can start volunteering at our centre. I have spoken to the people there about you and they are willing to help. They gave us a support letter for your bail."

Rafiq hadn't given a thought to such practical matters. "I've gotta go home," he said. He was not ready to talk about the future.

"Pray before you leave. It is time for the Isha namaaz."

—⁊⁊⁊—

When he got home, Ruksana told him that Ziram and Jameel had come to see him earlier in the evening.

"Ziram wants to talk to you."

"There is nothing to talk about."

"She wanted to know if she should inquire about a volunteer position for you at her workplace."

"Ammi, that would be the last option. Nagma Khala has offered me a paid position at her centre. I said no to her. I'll return to Wanderlust and meet Hameed tomorrow."

"All right, Beta, we are here to help you, don't run from us. But why did you go to Nagma Khala?"

He didn't reply.

Ruksana wasn't sure Hameed Surti would rehire Rafiq, but didn't want to voice her reservations and give Rafiq a reason to sulk. And she didn't approve of him working at Nagma's new centre. Restraining herself, mustering all the patience at her command, she smiled.

Rafiq knew what his mother's silence meant, but he didn't care. He went down to his room in the basement. He lay in bed, tired but unable to sleep. A little later, he heard his mother go up to her bedroom. He knew his parents wouldn't be sleeping any time soon. Rafiq suddenly wanted to go and embrace them both, but he didn't want to scare them. He was trapped. He wanted to be free and not hemmed in by his family, but he could never ignore them, never forget their sacrifices. He returned to the living room and turned on the TV. On one channel, a model in a bikini was selling cosmetics. She had an uncanny resemblance to Stacey, the former secretary and present wife of his employer, Hameed Surti.

Eighteen

Rafiq smiled when he thought of his employer, even though Hameed had often annoyed him at work. Hameed Surti, the owner of Wanderlust, a Brampton travel agency that specialized in customized adventure travel and boutique tourism to Turkey, Thailand and India, would greet him every morning with "Kyun Miyaan?" This was nothing more than an innocuous "What's up?" but Hameed emphasized the word *Miyaan*. In India, non-Muslims use that term—usually in derision—to describe Muslims. Rafiq, raised in Toronto, was clueless about it till Hameed himself explained it to Rafiq, and also shamelessly told him that he used it only to rile him.

"But you are a Muslim, too," Rafiq told him.

"When I choose to be . . . which is almost never."

Hameed often proclaimed that his being a Muslim was an accident of birth, explaining, "And I had no hand in it at all."

To prove his Canadian credentials, he would order a BLT sandwich with a double-double from the nearby Tim Horton's. Rafiq saw him as a bit of an oddball—smart but confused, and what was often referred to as a coconut—brown outside, white inside.

In the office were Hameed, Stacey, Rafiq and a few part-timers. Hameed had hired Rafiq from Sheridan's coop program. Initially Rafiq couldn't comprehend Hameed's disdain for religious faith, but as time went on he could see that his employer was actually tolerant of others' beliefs. Hameed had come from Bombay when he was in his thirties, and had successfully launched his travel business in a couple of years, offering tours to India.

He gave Rafiq a free hand in developing the company's website, and he transformed it from a static resource burner to an informative revenue earner. It had worked beyond Hameed's wildest wishes, and in gratitude, he gave Rafiq a raise, and also loaned him money for the down payment on the family's townhouse.

Hameed's wife, Stacey, was much younger than him and worked at Wanderlust three days a week. She had deep blue eyes, enhanced with cosmetics, and blonde hair. She wore a stud on her lips and her nose, and huge earrings. She also wore a diamond ring. Stacey's clothes were deliberately provocative: tight shirts that exposed her deep cleavage, tight miniskirts that revealed her panties when she crossed and uncrossed her long white legs. In her high-heeled shoes she towered above everyone. Stacey was aware of the effect she had on men. And she was, in particular, Rafiq's torment.

She would lean forward and Rafiq's pulse would race. When she sensed him gazing furtively at her, she would slowly uncross and cross back her legs. She would let out her sweet breath when close to him. At night he fantasized about her and masturbated; then hastily showered to cleanse himself of the guilt and asked forgiveness from God. Rafiq was like most desi boys and men—lust for the white women from afar but never manage to have a relationship with them.

Rafiq had been shy both in school and at Sheridan, and couldn't muster the courage to talk to girls, Sufiya was the exception, but it was she who had taken the initiative. When girls did speak to him, he would answer in monosyllables. He often imagined that Stacey was interested in him, but he knew that this wasn't true. He stopped thinking this when Hameed took him to lunch one day at an Indian restaurant and grandly announced that Stacey was pregnant.

Over time, Rafiq learned to hide his awkwardness in Stacey's presence. The trick was always to look at her face, or even at her earrings. Most of the time he succeeded. With news of her pregnancy he stopped fantasizing about her. By now he was deeply involved with Ghani Ahmed, and his dilemma was to find time for both Wanderlust and Ghani Ahmed's mission. Work at Wanderlust gave him a sense of authority and control, a sort of power, not over others, but over himself. But it wasn't his passion, not his junoon—his mission—as Nagma Khala termed it. His junoon was to serve Muslims.

His mother often spoke about getting him married, especially after

Ziram got married to Jameel, but Rafiq wasn't interested.

—◊◊—

When Rafiq reached the office complex on City Centre Drive, near Square One Mall in Mississauga; he stopped at the concierge desk in the downstairs lobby and announced his purpose. When the concierge called Wanderlust, the response was to ask him to wait. Rafiq was disappointed. He had expected to be called to the office immediately and greeted like a comrade. Hameed came down to meet him; obviously he didn't want him at Wanderlust.

His former employer, looking smart in a beige suede jacket over jeans, smiled at him, and then hugged him formally.

"Good to see you buddy, coffee?"

Rafiq nodded.

"Canada's gloomy these days," Hameed said, stepping outside. "And cold."

Rafiq hurried to keep pace with him. They crossed the road to a Starbucks.

"You're out on bail?" Hameed asked, and Rafiq nodded. "The cops came and asked questions," Hameed said.

"I didn't know that."

"Yeah, they wanted to know whether you used Wanderlust to do all that crazy stuff."

"I didn't."

"I know."

"Will you take me back?"

"No, buddy, I'm sorry. I run a business. If this gets into the media, I'll be done for. You're such a complete screwball."

"I'm not involved with any of this . . . what they accuse me of. I merely exchanged some emails."

"Even if I believed you, I can't help you right now."

"How about if I work from home?"

"Look, Rafiq, I like you and your work. But I can't have you back."

They lapsed into silence. There wasn't anything left to talk about.

Hameed knew losing Rafiq might adversely affect his business in the short term, but retaining him would definitely destroy it.

"Call me when your court case is over," he said.

—⁓—

Dejected, Rafiq returned home. His parents didn't have to ask him to how the meeting with Hameed went. He dozed off on the couch in the living room, and woke to the smell of a potent curry that Ammi was cooking. She had opened the kitchen window but that only let a cold draught in without letting the curry odour out. When Ziram and Jameel arrived, Rafiq got up and closed the window. His mother turned and smiled at him.

"Hameed doesn't want me, so I'm taking up Nagma Khala's offer," he said.

"Are you sure? You'll be back with those people . . . " Ziram began, but Rafiq interrupted her. "They'll pay. Your centre won't," he said edgily, but then cooled down. "Besides, we need money."

"You will seek that woman's help but not ours?" Ruksana said, her voice breaking.

Rafiq remained quiet.

"You'll have a better future at our centre," Ziram said.

"Who's going to pay the mortgage until the trial is over?"

"You don't have to worry about that. We'll manage," Jameel replied.

"I'm starting work at Kartar's shop," Abdul said. "Your mother is planning to apply at the medicine factory."

"This doesn't make any sense. If both of you can work, why can't I?" Rafiq said.

Abdul couldn't contain his irritation. "You want to go back to those half-wit fanatics so that we sit at home and see you destroy yourself all over again? You are not doing that. I'm not letting you do that!"

"Abba, what makes you so sure they are fanatics?"

"Beta, I have seldom interfered in your life and I don't want to start now. But this time, listen to what we are saying. It is for your own good."

Abdul walked over from the chair and put his hand on his son's shoulder. He looked at him pleadingly.

"OK, Abba. I will go to Ziram's centre tomorrow." He didn't want to argue any more.

—⚉—

That night, in his desperation to fall asleep, Rafiq thought he would take a couple of sleeping pills and rummaged through the washroom medicine cabinet looking for them. He didn't find any. His parents never took sleeping pills; they were used to their insomniac lives. He wondered whether his sleeplessness had started after he got to know Ghani Ahmed. Before he let that man into his life, Rafiq never had any trouble falling asleep.

In the morning, Ammi came to wake him up for the namaaz but he didn't get up. Later, he was annoyed with himself for allowing his laziness to keep him from his resolve to pray every morning. He wore his formal work clothes to go to Ziram's centre. He wasn't sure he wanted to wear a tie so he took one with him, just in case Ziram or Jameel suggested that he should. Abdul told him to take the car but he didn't want to. He put on his black leather jacket and stepped out. He stuffed his hands in his coat pockets, put his head down and walked briskly down the road; however, the gusty wind defeated him. He returned and took the car keys.

At the Malton Settlement and Community Centre, Ziram took him to the visitors' meeting room, which had a row of desktops.

"Update your resume and keep it ready. Mike should be here by ten," his sister told him.

"Do you want me to come back later?"

"No. I'll take you to see him as soon as he's here."

Rafiq examined the ageing, bulky desktop computers; they were so ancient that some of the newer software wouldn't run on them. He checked the centre's website: its ancient coding was cumbersome and hampered accessibility. There was so much he could do here, like enabling access to the website through cellphones, and tablet computers that were soon to hit the market. Rafiq tried to check his email, but access to the internet was through a password; annoyed, he began typing his résumé. He was still upset that Hameed had declined to take him back.

While he was at it, Ziram came and took him to Mike's office, knocked softly on the door, and led him in. A man, probably in his mid-forties, sat behind a desk wearing a full-sleeved white shirt. He was peering at a sheet of paper. He looked up, took off his reading glasses, and smiled at Ziram.

"Good morning, Ziram. Ah, yes. I remember. Your brother."

"Yes, Mike, here he is. Meet Rafiq, and Rafiq this is Mike McLaughlin, our centre's executive director."

Mike walked out from behind his desk and shook hands with Rafiq.

"Ah! A firm handshake," he said. Mike made rapid judgements about people he met. It was part of his job dealing with newcomers. About Rafiq, his first impressions were positive. Not the limp handshake of an immigrant. He is Canadian, most likely born and raised here.

"Come sit." Mike offered him a chair across from his desk. Ziram took this as her cue and left.

"Give me a moment; I have to send an email," Mike said, putting on his glasses and peering at his screen.

Mike's work desk was a bit too neat to be effective. A document holder with a few files, and some basic stationery and office items, no paper, no general disorder common to a work desk. There was a water bottle and a glass near the monitor. A framed family photo: a wife and two kids. The kids resembled the wife more than him, Rafiq thought.

Behind Mike's desk was a large window, which seemed odd to Rafiq. Mike saw the inside of a monotonous office, but his visitors got a great view of the street outside, lined with trees, which had turned a splendid gold and red. The wall next to the window had a framed photograph of a house in the woods.

Mike turned his chair to face Rafiq. "Let us get a few irritants out of the way, shall we?" he asked.

Rafiq tried to smile.

"You're going to start as a volunteer, so there's no pay. You're filling in for the person who looks after our website, during his absence." Mike ticked off with his pencil a checklist on a notepad. "Any questions?"

Rafiq cleared his throat. "Well, you know about my case," he said nervously.

"Yes, your sister told me about it. We're not employing you, so that shouldn't be a concern right now."

"And after the case concludes, can I get a regular job here?"

"We'll cross that bridge when, or rather, *if* we come to it. You can start today if you want."

"Okay," Rafiq replied with a shy smile.

Mike gave a wide grin, got up and came over to shake hands again, and returned to his desk. His tone and too-friendly demeanour had made Rafiq uneasy. He wanted to ask him why he was doing him this favour. He realized that he needed to park himself somewhere till his court case was sorted out, but he found Mike arrogant. Rafiq felt humiliated. In the few moments it took Rafiq to reach the reception area from Mike's office, he decided that he didn't want to work at the Malton centre.

"So how did it go?" Ziram asked him. She was waiting for him at reception.

Rafiq looked at the receptionist, who was busy on the phone. He whispered to his sister: "I don't want to work here. The guy was nice to me when you were with me, but turned nasty after you left the room."

"You should take some time before you decide," Ziram said.

"No, I'm going to meet Nagma Khala right now," Rafiq said. He was determined more than ever to start working. He was hurt by Hameed's rejection but now he felt defiant after his experience with Mike.

Nineteen

The traffic on the 401 was light. He pulled out his cellphone and called Nagma Khala.

"Everything OK?" she asked.

"Khala, I'm coming over to meet you. I want to start working at the new centre."

"Yes OK, you come over."

Rafiq fiddled with the knobs to lower the volume on the radio, which came on automatically when he started the car. A local FM station was playing an old Hindi movie song, one he had heard his mother hum sometimes, remembering her Teli Gali, while cooking. When the song ended, the host made an abrupt announcement in Hindustani about a terrorist attack in Bombay—a handful of gunmen had fired at the crowds at Bombay's main train terminal, and another group had seized the five-star Taj Mahal Hotel in the city. He remembered seeing it at the Gateway of India.

Immediately he felt his stomach churn. Rafiq recalled how he had agreed to go along with Ghani Ahmed's plan, blanking out what it actually meant—killing real people. He realized the implications of that only when he went scouting around Toronto for locations for Ghani Ahmed. And had it not been for the mother wearing a hijab and her kids at the food court in Square One Mall, he would probably still be involved with Ghani Ahmed. The killing of innocent people; people who were like him, his sister, his mother and father; people who had nothing to do with Canada's involvement in Afghanistan or anywhere else, who just managed to eke out their lives and give their children better futures, just as his own parents had done. It could have been Abba and Ammi at the mall, or Ziram and Jameel with their baby. He had balked at the idea of turning into a crazed murderer and backed out.

He wouldn't have been any different from the terrorists who had attacked Bombay. He asked himself if he was any different from them even now; after all, he had been an integral part of Ghani Ahmed's plan. Would he be applauding the terrible news from Bombay, as Ghani Ahmed would surely be doing right now? These Bombay terrorists too would have surveyed their locations prior to the attack and the siege. Luckily he had had the sense to quit. He could only attribute his conscience to his upbringing. Abba and Ammi had values, and they themselves had cared for the poor of any religious faith when they were based in Bombay. They too had been victims of fanatics. And his understanding of Islam had come from his mother and Nagma Khala, not from Ghani Ahmed.

He also realized how his own situation must seem to others. He had to admit that it was bad. Why should anyone now believe him if he told them that he had backed out of Ghani Ahmed's plan? There was no proof. Seized by the similarities between him and the Bombay terrorists, Rafiq found it hard to focus on the road. He began to sweat.

There had been so many attacks inside Bombay in the last few years. Rafiq had often justified them as revenge, just retribution in response to injustices against Muslims in India. His father didn't agree with him; instead he bemoaned the end of Indian secularism. In despair, Abdul would either say, "You are ignorant," or "Islam doesn't justify or condone random killing of the innocent. Read the Quran yourself! Ask your mother! Isn't she a devout Muslim?"

The radio played a new number. It was about Bombay and he had never heard it before. Rafiq took the Black Creek exit from the highway and drove down Lawrence Avenue West. Nagma Khala was waiting for him outside her building, at Caledonia. She smiled and got in the car and Rafiq lowered the radio's volume. She wore a dark red woollen jacket and a red hijab that rather stood out on her, and smelled like her kitchen.

"What have you told them at the centre?" Rafiq asked.

"They know everything," Nagma said.

"And they've agreed to take me on?"

"Yes. Kulsum is the manager. A nice young woman. What is the matter, what happened?"

He didn't want to tell her that his parents would get upset to know he was going with her and planning to work with her at the centre. They wouldn't see things the same way as Nagma Khala did, especially now, with this terrorist attack in Bombay.

"Khala, I just heard on the radio that terrorists have attacked a railway station and a hotel in Bombay."

"Oh no, now the TV people will go crazy, and Muslims will have to keep saying sorry," Nagma said. She shuffled uneasily in the seat.

"Do you think that the centre may not want to engage me because of this?"

"What has that got to do with you . . . ?" Nagma exclaimed and then realized what he was saying. "We don't have to talk about it."

There was another update on the radio. The terrorists had entered another hotel and taken hostages.

"This is bad," Nagma Khala murmured, shaking her head.

By the time they reached the centre in Thorncliffe Park, all that Rafiq could think about was the attacks in Bombay and his family's reaction to it. He was convinced that his parents, his sister, her husband, all of them would object to the idea of him working with Nagma Khala. Before getting out of the car, he called home. His father answered, although Rafiq had wanted it to be his Ammi.

"Watch the news," Rafiq said shortly. "There's been a terrorist attack on Bombay."

"We know. Where are you?"

"I'm with Nagma Khala at the centre. I'll call you later."

—⟶⟵—

The centre was in an old but well maintained building that had been a residence earlier. A corridor led to a staircase going up to the second floor, which had rooms on either side. To the right was a large office with a desk to match. A young woman was furiously keyboarding. Nagma greeted the woman with "As salaam Aleikum" and introduced Rafiq.

The woman got up and greeted them.

"Waleikum salaam. I am Kulsum. Please sit."

She was wearing a light grey shirt and dark brown trousers.

"I'll be free in a moment," Kulsum said and smiled. She then quickly finished her work.

She looked up and took off her glasses. She was a petite, poised woman not much older than him, and Rafiq felt immediately at ease. She didn't have an accent.

"Nagma told me about your situation and I've spoken to the board of directors. They are OK with it."

"Before we get any further, I must tell you something," Rafiq said, clearing his throat. "I just heard on the radio when we were coming here that there's been a terrorist attack in Bombay. I wanted to tell this to you upfront, so you know of it before you decide anything."

She smiled. "I've heard the news too. But thank you for bringing it up. I don't think that should be a problem. None of the board members has called me to stop your appointment so far, and I'm sure some of them would've heard about it. I'll let you know of any developments in case their decision changes. Do you want to discuss your work? Nagma must've told you that we pay slightly over minimum wage."

Rafiq's cellphone, turned to silent mode, was buzzing furiously in his pocket. He wanted to ignore it but when Kulsum said, "You can take the call," he excused himself and answered. It was Abba.

"Beta, you come home right now. Your mother is very worried about you."

"Abba, I'm OK. I'll call you in a bit. I'm in a meeting."

"What are you doing at Nagma's centre?" Abba asked, his tone bitter, and more questions followed, in a rush, unceasing. "Why did you go back on your promise? Why are you with Nagma? What are you doing at the centre? Who is in charge there? What else does the centre do? Do you know everything that they do at that place? Is it a madrassa? Do you even know what you are doing? You are on bail! Stay away from those fanatics. See what is happening in Bombay!"

Rafiq couldn't respond to this barrage, and he knew that even if he patiently gave the answers to all the questions, his dad would raise more. Nothing was going to change his dad's mind.

"Your Ammi isn't well, she will get worse now because of you," Abba said.

Rafiq ended the call and looked at Kulsum and Nagma Khala uncomprehendingly. Ammi could have had a breakdown but she could well be all right. It was possible that Abba was making it all up. In the past, his dad and his sister had used his weakness for his mother, and her weakness for him, to get them to do as they wished. Rafiq was sweating profusely, and shivering.

The two women observed him anxiously.

Rafiq took a deep breath to calm himself. Then another. It didn't help. He was convinced he was having a heart attack. He staggered back to the chair and crashed into it, clutching the hand rest. Kulsum got up and hurried to get him a glass of water. He clutched at it and tried to steady his nerves, but failed and spilled water down his jacket and onto his trousers.

"There's a couch in the other room. He can lie down till he feels better," Kulsum said, her eyes wide with fear.

Nagma sat rooted to her chair.

Rafiq shouted, "I want to go home. Take me home. Call Abba, my dad, he'll have to come and get me, I can't drive!" He was shaking. Nagma sprang up and led him to the other room. She covered him with her red jacket.

Abdul answered Nagma's call, but handed the phone to Ruksana when he didn't recognize her voice. Nagma told Ruksana that Rafiq was having a panic attack and wanted to return home. "I don't drive," she said. "Someone will have to come here to take us back."

"I will ask Ziram. Saabji can't come because Rafiq has the car. You wait with him. Ziram will call you," Ruksana said. Then, turning to Abdul, and hiding her mounting anxiety, she said, "Rafiq is having a panic attack; he is asking for you to go there and get him back home. Ziram should go." Seeing the alarm and fear in his eyes, she calmed him. "Steady your nerves. I can't handle both of you panicking."

Abdul couldn't stop being surprised at his wife's measured responses. She never reacted hysterically in such situations, never lost control. She had the unique ability of quietly steering them away from the precipice.

"Ammi, it'll take me forever in the traffic," Ziram groaned when her mother told her to fetch Rafiq and Nagma from the centre.

Ruksana ignored her grumbling and warned her, "I don't want to hear a word from you. You understand? Not a word. Just go there and get your brother back."

She hung up and, turning to Abdul, said in a severe tone, "And once he is here, we are not watching the news. Is that clear?" He wanted to tell her not to treat him like an insensitive imbecile, but kept quiet. They continued to watch the news in silence. The Taj Mahal hotel, one of Bombay's prominent landmarks, was on fire.

Ziram called Rafiq to get the centre's address and Nagma gave it to her, then she texted to Jameel about where she was going, and drove off.

"Why's this happening to me? What the fuck have I done?" she muttered to herself as she stomped on the gas pedal. "He won't let anyone live in peace," she muttered again, but then calmed down.

Her doctor had told her not to get aggravated over small things. "It'll harm the foetus." That thought calmed her nerves and she had a change of heart. She was being selfish, thinking only of herself, when she was part of a loving family.

A huge tragedy was potentially waiting to happen. Rafiq was probably dying. Even if he survived, he would in all likelihood spend many years in jail, and become a mental wreck. But all she could think about was the effect all this would have on her life and on Jameel's promotion. It was wrong to blame her brother. He was going through severe problems and he needed all the help he could get from his family. Ziram knew that every little thing that was going wrong now would adversely affect her life and Jameel's career, but right now there was nothing she could do, and she had to focus on helping Rafiq. She had decided to help when all of this began, and she didn't have a choice but to stick to it.

Kulsum introduced herself when Ziram bustled in, and led her upstairs to Rafiq. He looked up from the couch where Nagma was gently massaging his head. They spent a moment sizing each other up. Ziram wanted to strangle both him and the unctuous Nagma. Rafiq was upset to see her and not his father because she would grumble and swear and berate him. Right now he wanted to be understood and treated gently. He felt like a child.

"Let's get going," she said tonelessly and helped him get up. With Nagma's help she got him down the stairs and into the car. Nagma too got in.

"We'll come to get his car later," Ziram told Kulsum.

—⁂—

Ruksana came out and stood by the door when she heard the car enter the driveway. She had instructed Abdul to stay inside. Nagma held Rafiq and helped him out of the car.

"Do you want water?" Ruksana asked Rafiq. He shook his head, eased himself on to the couch and shut his eyes.

"Beta, should we call a doctor?" Abdul asked, but Ruksana motioned him to keep quiet.

"He heard the news on the radio, and then when Abdul bhaisaab called he couldn't stop shivering. I didn't know what to do," Nagma said.

"It's all right, Nagma," Ruksana said and took her hand. "You did the right thing."

"I'm going down to my room," Rafiq said, and Ruksana followed him.

"I will go home," Nagma said, hesitantly.

"Stay for dinner," Ziram said without actually meaning it.

"No. I will take the bus," Nagma said, checking her wristwatch. She didn't want to stay.

Abdul switched on the television, but kept the volume low so that Rafiq wouldn't hear it. He wasn't sure how his son could possibly be disturbed by it, but he didn't want another futile argument with his wife. The siege was already into several hours. Bombay had turned into a battlefield, with buildings ablaze, and pitched gun battles between terrorists and the Indian police. Hundreds of people had been killed. Abdul flipped channels. By now they were all talking about nothing else. The CBC reported that Canadian citizens had been taken hostage, and a Jewish Rabbi's family was being held hostage in a synagogue near the hotel.

"Get your mother; we were watching the news," Abdul told Ziram.

He wanted Ruksana beside him to share his despair. His Bombay was being destroyed and only she could understand what that meant to him.

In the basement, Ziram saw a familiar sight. Rafiq was sprawled on the bed and Ammi was sitting beside him, doing nothing. She had grown up seeing this—her mother mollycoddling her brother—and it had always made her mad. It exasperated her today.

"Ammi, Abba is calling you to watch TV with him. Rafiq, you'll also feel better if you come up and sit with us," Ziram said.

"Yes, Beta, Ziram is right," Ruksana said.

Ziram shook her head in disgust. Her mother's tone was more suited for a six-year-old boy, not a twenty-year-old man.

Soon Jameel arrived, and saw everyone looking intensely worried. He sat on the couch and pulled his laptop from his bag.

Ruksana gave Jameel a half smile. "It has got real bad, hasn't it?" she said.

"Oh yes, looks like it could go on for hours."

Rafiq's mind was a war zone too. His family was supporting him and sympathizing with him, but he could well imagine what they were thinking. It was what he was thinking about himself. That he was no different than those gun-toting maniacs who had taken over Bombay, the city of his birth, and were killing innocent people.

Ruksana knew what her son was going through. She came to him, held his face in her hands.

"You are not like them," she whispered.

Rafiq broke down, sobbing loudly. It was hard for the rest of the family to watch.

"Come with us to our apartment. We'll watch a movie," Jameel suggested.

"Yes, that'll take your mind off all this," Ziram said.

Rafiq nodded. Abdul and Ruksana were not quite sure whether he should leave home so soon after his panic attack, but they were happy he had agreed to accompany his sister and her husband.

Twenty

The panoramic view from Ziram and Jameel's west-facing apartment was glorious in the evenings especially during spring and summer, when the sun took its time to set and a glow spread over the horizon, and now in the fall, when it was already dark outside, and the shimmering lights from the tall buildings and the traffic below looked magical.

Ziram laid out the dinner but Rafiq was restless.

"Come, let's have dinner," Jameel said, giving him a gentle pat on his shoulder.

"I've got a headache," Rafiq said.

"There's aspirin in the cabinet in the washroom," Ziram said.

Rafiq went to the washroom and rummaged through a box in the cabinet by the mirror. It had all sorts of medicines, including a small box containing strips of sleeping pills.

At the table he asked Jameel, "You take sleeping pills?"

"Sometimes."

"Do they help?"

"Yes, generally."

"And they are addictive. These days he can't sleep without taking those damn pills," Ziram said.

"I should try, too. I haven't been sleeping well," Rafiq said.

"Get a doctor to prescribe you some," Jameel said cautiously, glancing at Ziram, not sure where the conversation was leading to.

After dinner they settled down to watch a movie but Jameel soon started work on his laptop answering emails, and Ziram got busy with her cellphone. It was late evening and they had to be at work the next morning, so Rafiq asked them to drop him home. Before leaving, he went to the washroom and pilfered three strips of the sleeping pills.

—⁓—

Ammi and Abba were in their bedroom when Rafiq reached home. He changed into his nightclothes—a t-shirt and sweatpants—and pushed out all the capsules from one of the strips of sleeping pills. That should be enough, he thought. Now that he had the means, he had to make up his mind whether he really wanted to end his life. Islam forbade suicide, but he would beg forgiveness from Allah, who was merciful. His death was the best solution for everybody, for all the problems he had caused.

He poured water into a glass and gulped down all the capsules. He then tried to sleep, but couldn't. He desperately wanted to be at peace with himself; his mind was like the raging sea at high tide that he had seen in Bombay. Hours passed and he was still alert. He stared at the ceiling, switched on the bedside lamp, got up and took all of the capsules from the second strip. He hid the other strip in his desk drawer. He would be dead by the time they discovered it.

It was 1:08 a.m., he checked. He hoped to fall asleep soon and never wake up, but he was still not feeling sleepy. He took that as a sign from Allah.

His mood swung the other way. He was gripped by serious doubts about his decision to end his life. He didn't have to die. Everything could be changed. Nothing was inevitable. He realized it was this strong and determined inner urge and the will to live that had prevented him from falling asleep, kept him alert all the time.

His death would cause his family more pain. His situation wasn't all that bad. The worst that could possibly happen was a maximum sentence by the court and a long term behind bars. But there was hope because he had been given bail. He could start his own consultancy and maybe Hameed would give him some business. His problems were short-term, not permanent, and eventually he would find solutions. Abba and Ammi might need to work temporarily, or Ziram could help them with the mortgage for now and he would pay her back later. He could get married—Nagma Khala had once offered to help him find "a good namaazi girl."

He wanted to live. But now the pills were making him drowsy.

Rafiq went to the washroom and splashed water on his face. In the mirror he searched his face for any adverse effects of the sleeping pills. If he had his laptop, he could have Googled for an antidote or something like that. What did they do in such cases? Should he wake up his parents, or call Ziram, or call 911. Maybe he should call Nagma Khala. He checked the clock again. It was now nearly 4:00 a.m. Ammi should be getting up any time soon, and Abba was probably still awake sitting on his red armchair mulling.

Rafiq went up to the living room and waited for his mother to come down for her namaaz. He was afraid that she would find him dead or unconscious. He turned on the TV, muting the sound. There was nothing on but shopping or evangelists preaching with passion. He found a movie that he had seen before, about fast cars and brawny men, and women with very few clothes. He clicked the info button on the remote: the movie was *The Fast and the Furious*. He heard his mother coming down the stairs.

By now he was barely able to keep his eyes open.

"Ammi, come here," he forced himself to say. His voice was a slurred whisper.

She flicked on the living room lights and saw him.

"Why are you up so early?"

He tried to answer, but only his throat moved. Ruksana hurried to his side, her eyes wide with fear.

"Call 911, I've taken sleeping pills," he said, softly. And then he closed his eyes.

On the television a car flew across an intersection and crashed into another one. Ruksana turned it off. She was terrified but had to keep calm. She shouted for her husband. "Abdul, Abdul, jaldi, quickly come down—fast!"

Upstairs Abdul was in the washroom, ready to go to sleep, when he heard Ruksana. He was surprised she was calling him by name. She always called him Saabji. He hurried down with just a towel wrapped around his waist.

"Kya hua?" he asked and cried out in anguish when he saw Rafiq lying still on the couch, Ruksana caressing his forehead.

"What has happened to him?"

"Saabji . . . Rafiq . . . call 911 . . . he took sleeping pills."

The towel slipped from Abdul's waist. Ruksana looked at her husband, bare-bodied, vulnerable, so vulnerable. She lost her composure. A deep sob tore at her throat.

Abdul picked up the towel, and wrapped it back around his waist. He couldn't think what to do.

"Call 911!" Ruksana said above her sobs. She was finding it hard to breathe.

Abdul grabbed the telephone, and in accented, broken sentences explained the situation and gave the address to the operator.

"Is he breathing?" asked the operator.

"Yes," he said and listened to her instructions. When she hung up, Abdul ran to the bedroom to put on some clothes.

"Call Ziram," Ruksana said when he came back.

Jameel answered the phone. Abdul told him to get Ziram and rush over. Then he ran to the kitchen and got a glass of water. "Splash water on his face, splash water," he said. It didn't make any difference; Rafiq seemed to be in a coma. Abdul called Kartar and asked him to come over. The neighbours came, shivering in their night clothes.

"What time?" Kartar asked.

"I don't know. She saw him about five minutes ago."

They heard the ambulance stop outside. It had arrived without sirens. Two men and a woman in uniform entered hurriedly. One of the paramedics checked Rafiq's pulse, pushed opened his eyelids, checked his pupils.

"Do you know how many pills he swallowed?" the man asked.

Ruksana shook her head.

"You're his parents?" he asked Abdul.

"Yes."

While one of the paramedics told Ruksana to look for the pill bottle, the others brought in a stretcher. They lifted Rafiq onto it.

"We're taking him to Trillium, you two can come with us," the woman said to the parents.

"Wait for Ziram and tell them to come to the hospital," Ruksana said to Harminder. "And get my salwaar-kameez."

She grabbed an overcoat and got into the ambulance with Abdul. Just then Jameel and Ziram arrived. Ziram ran out of the car and hugged her mother; both broke down holding each other. Abdul shouted at Ruksana, "There's no time for this, let's go!" In the back of the ambulance they sat crouched on a cramped bench next to Rafiq. The ambulance moved swiftly and quietly. The sirens stayed silent, but some of the neighbours from the adjoining homes were standing by their doors watching them.

At the entrance to the Emergency department they clambered out in the chilly dawn. They had to run, panting, to keep pace with the paramedics wheeling in Rafiq. This was the second time Ruksana had been in a big hospital, the first was when Dhinmant had died, and she couldn't help but notice the contrast. The hospital in Bombay was overcrowded and grimy. This place was deserted but for a few members of the staff, and it was clean.

A doctor who, judging from his accent and his curly, jet-black hair, was from somewhere in the Middle East, told them to wait in the lounge, where he asked them how many pills Rafiq had taken and when. They didn't know, Abdul said. Ziram and Jameel arrived with a fresh pair of salwaar-kameez for Ruksana, who went to the washroom to change. The doctor had left by the time she returned.

"Did the doctor say what they will be doing?" she asked Abdul, and then glanced at Jameel. "Shouldn't they be pumping everything out of his stomach?"

"Ammi, they know what to do," Ziram said calmly.

"Beta, this is standard procedure. They should do it before asking us anything."

"Where is Kartar?" Abdul asked.

"We were in a hurry, so I told them not to come right now, they can come later. No point every one being here unnecessarily," Ziram said.

—ᴍ—

Ruksana whispered into Abdul's ear that she wanted to offer the namaaz. She expected him to be annoyed and object. To her surprise he agreed. She performed the ablutions and returned with her head covered by her dupatta. She walked to the corner of the lounge and prayed. Breaking her resolve of not asking Allah for anything, she pleaded, "Let him live, let him live . . . "

"I hope Allah listens to your prayers," Abdul said when she returned. He put his arm around her. She hesitantly rested her head on his shoulder. They had wasted so many years in futile arguments. But now finally they were together, united in their grief, their animosities abandoned, realizing their common bond and their need for each other in this the worst moment of their lives.

"He is not going to die. He wants to live. Otherwise he wouldn't have told me," she said, speaking softly. He nodded. "Of course." Ruksana's determined look told him she would do what it would take to save her son, and she was a tough woman, as Abdul knew. But he wondered what even she could do.

She had successfully defied destiny many times before. Destiny— manzil, what they called their house. Was this what her—their—destiny was going to be? She had fled from Sarhupur to save herself; fled from Bombay to save the family. Had fate finally caught up with her? In Bombay, she would have marched straight to the head of the hospital and demanded answers. Here, they both hesitated, not sure of what to do. Ziram and Jameel seemed to rely on the system and go with the flow, rather than actively seek out information.

"We've pumped your son's stomach and given him an antidote to the sleeping pills," said a sleepy-looking male nurse. "We're closely monitoring him. Not all of you need to be here now. Our visiting hours are from noon to eight p.m."

Abdul cleared his throat and said, "Our son was out on bail."

The nurse looked surprised. "Why was he in prison?" he asked.

Abdul looked at Ziram for help, and she looked at Jameel.

"You'll have to inform the Peel police," Jameel said.

The nurse nodded. "The discharge procedure will change. We'll talk to the cops," he said and then slowly walked back.

Ruksana sighed, and Ziram held her hand. "Ammi, he'll be fine. We should get going now; call us when he gets up, or if you need something," she said.

"Tell Nagma. She will be upset if we don't tell her."

"She'll run straight to the hospital," Ziram said.

"That is OK, she needs to know," Ruksana said firmly.

Abdul and Ruksana watched the empty lounge after Ziram and Jameel had left.

"This is Canada, nothing can disrupt routine," Ruksana whispered, and Abdul nodded vigorously.

The hospital was slowly coming alive. They went to the information desk to check if they could see Rafiq. The woman, waiting for her shift to end, pointed the way distractedly. Hidden under bed sheets, Rafiq appeared small and fragile on the bed. The white sheet that covered him rose and fell gently. A saline tube was stuck to his arm and two tubes were inserted in his nostrils. Ruksana touched his forehead with the back of her palm to check if he was running a fever.

—⚏—

"Khala, sorry to wake you up so early," Ziram said into her cellphone.

"Kaun? Ziram?"

"Yes, Khala."

"Is everything all right?" Nagma asked. "Is Rafiq OK?"

"Ya Allah," she gasped when Ziram told her.

"Khala, he's going to be just fine; don't cry. Ammi and Abba are with him, he's out of danger."

"Thank God. I will go to the hospital right now."

"How will you go? Trillium is quite far from your place. Come and see him when he's back home."

"I will take a taxi."

Nagma wanted to pray for Rafiq before leaving for the hospital but she wanted to be with Rafiq even more. She shoved her prayer beads into a woollen bag, changed into a fresh salwaar-kameez and tied her hair inside a black hijab. She stuffed five twenty-dollar bills down the front of her kameez and grabbed her red jacket on her way out, remembering she had worn it when she had accompanied Rafiq to the centre in Thorncliffe. She reached the hospital in fifteen minutes.

The cabbie rolled his eyes when she shoved her hand inside her kameez to fish out the money. He gave a grimace as he took the bills, moist with her sweat, and drove away disgusted. Nagma found Ruksana and Abdul sitting listlessly in the lounge. Abdul greeted her with an adaab. Ruksana hugged her and wept.

"He wants to live," Ruksana tried to speak in between her sobs. She was convinced that Nagma would forever judge her as a failed mother.

"Allah will protect him," Nagma replied.

Abdul shifted uncomfortably in his chair and then got up to go to the washroom. He had surprised himself by remaining calm during the crisis, perhaps because he had known all along that something like this was inevitable. He returned to the lounge, reflecting on the relationship that Ruksana, Nagma, and Rafiq shared. Both the women were responsible in so many ways for Rafiq's transformation into a zealot.

Ruksana had been blinded by her motherly love and couldn't or didn't want to see the obvious problems with their son. Everyone in the community knew and liked him, but he had no friends, and Ruksana didn't find that of concern at all. She argued that he would "straighten out" once he was settled in a job and had gotten married.

Nagma had an inexplicable bond with his family. They rarely saw her, but she was ever present in their conversations. He remembered Ziram telling them once that Nagma was worried that Rafiq was turning too deeply religious to ever marry. This was when he was under Ghani Ahmed's influence. Dismayed, Ruksana had asked Rafiq about it, but he had replied that he wasn't thinking about marriage, didn't want the responsibilities that came with it, he wanted to work and be financially secure first. "And I'm too young to marry," he had said.

Abdul found it ironic that Ruksana was now seeking solace from Nagma. After Rafiq's arrest, she had blamed Nagma for turning her son into a fanatic. But to Abdul there was no difference between Ruksana's piety and Nagma's religiosity. He wondered at the uneasy relationship they had, what Nagma thought about the family, especially Ruksana. He was certain Nagma loved Rafiq as a son.

He thought of Ziram and Jameel, how they had unselfishly rallied around the family. He was pleased with their support, it had been essential.

Twenty-one

Ravindar was at his desk when Kartar called to tell him about Rafiq's attempted suicide. Ravindar said he would visit the hospital, but Kartar wasn't sure he should do that.

"You will remind them of his arrest."

"Uncle, you know I did what was right," Ravindar protested.

"Just let them be for now."

Ravindar called police headquarters to inform the investigators on the case about Rafiq. They had already dispatched two officers to the hospital. Ravindar had actually felt uneasy that his decision to call in his seniors that day when the emails were discovered had led to Rafiq's arrest, but he had no doubt that he had done the right thing. Hundreds if not thousands would have been killed had the conspiracy succeeded, and it could all still happen because Ghani Ahmed was at large.

What Ravindar lacked in empathy, he made up with efficiency. He came to Canada with his parents in the 1980s when he was a teenager. He did well in school but didn't want to study further, being eager to start working so that he could help his parents. Eventually, after a police course when he was admitted to the force, he got his parents to retire.

Kartar was a distant cousin of Ravindar's mother. To him Ravindar was like a son, and he had often helped his parents without making it seem like charity. Through his uncle, Ravindar came to know Abdul and his family. Ravindar had always found Abdul fascinating—articulate, mild-mannered, and dignified. He had been a leader of people back in India.

A little later Ravindar called his uncle again. "Tell them I'll be going to the hospital to see them."

Kartar thought for a moment and then said, "Beta, I will call them, and you call them too. And when you meet them, share their sorrow, don't ask questions."

"I won't ask anything. I just want to meet them."

To Kartar's surprise, Abdul agreed to let Ravindar come and meet them. "Let him come if he wants to. He can't undo what has happened . . . Though Ruksana won't like it." Abdul glanced briefly at Ruksana. "But if he wants to come, let him."

"Let him come," she said resignedly, when Abdul told her about Ravindar's intent. She turned to Nagma and said, "That policeman is coming to meet us."

"Should I leave?"

"No, no, you stay. You are family," Ruksana said.

Nagma smiled and became tearful; for the first time Ruksana had acknowledged her as family.

Waiting for his uncle to call him, Ravindar was anxious and sweating under his uniform. He lowered the blinds of his windows and the unexpected brightness of the sun on a cold morning made him blink. He fiddled with the papers on his desk. He wasn't sure of what to say to Abdul and his wife. Finally, after what seemed like forever, his uncle called and said, "They are waiting for you."

Before he arrived, two other police officers had reached the hospital.

"You are Rafiq Latif's family?" one of them asked Abdul. He nodded in response.

"We'll be staying around." They briskly walked to the emergency room, where Rafiq was.

Abdul looked at them warily as they walked away, then turned to Ruksana.

"Saabji, this must be their procedure," she said calmly.

Abdul was mentally rehearsing what not to say to Ravindar. He repeatedly glanced down the corridor. The growing bustle was better than the eerie silence that had enveloped the place earlier. When they saw Ravindar walking up the corridor, both Abdul and Ruksana stiffened. His heels clicked sharply on the tiled floor. Ruksana lost her composure and clenched her fists under her dupatta. Nagma was both fascinated and scared.

Ravindar stood before Abdul, who didn't get up to greet him.

"How's he?" Ravindar asked.

"Out of danger."

Ravindar didn't know what more to say. When Nagma asked him to sit, he nodded but continued to stand, and then gingerly sat beside Abdul. He, too, had rehearsed what he was going to say.

"I've come to share your grief. I'm really sorry about what happened," he said, his voice strained.

Abdul took in a deep breath and spoke slowly, "My son is not a criminal. You and your system may treat him as one, but he is merely misguided. I don't say this because he is my son. He needs help, not a prison term."

"Sir, I don't think it's that simple," Ravindar said, keeping his tone soft. "You do realize that he is involved in a big conspiracy."

"Rafiq told me that he wasn't actually involved, except initially."

Ravindar was about to say something but checked himself.

Then Ruksana spoke, her shrill tone betraying the anxiety and anger that she had so wanted to conceal. "My son is not a killer. They picked on him at school. His fault is that he is a Muslim. They tortured him in prison also," she said.

Ravindar preferred to keep quiet. When the silence became unbearable, he said, "We must focus on getting Ghani Ahmed. If his men contact you, we want you to tell us."

"Yes, of course, we have nothing to hide," Abdul said emphatically.

Ruksana said, "Saabji, we don't want to be involved with any of this anymore."

"Ruksana, I will help Ravindar catch Ghani Ahmed if I can," Abdul said with conviction, then turning to Ravindar, he said, "You have my word."

After a moment of silence when everyone looked around uncomfortably, Abdul spoke, slowly but firmly: "I hold both Canada and Ghani Ahmed responsible for what has happened to Rafiq. I'm too old to leave Canada but I can certainly help get Ghani Ahmed arrested."

Ravindar wasn't sure whether he should stay any longer. He got up, awkwardly nodded, and walked down the corridor. His admiration for Abdul had risen a few notches higher after this meeting, even if he didn't agree with his views.

—◇◇◇—

It was almost noon and they had been in the hospital for several hours. Abdul was exhausted, especially after the tense meeting with Ravindar. He got up from the chair with some effort; sitting for long hours even on stuffed chairs was uncomfortable.

"Let's go and see if he is awake," Abdul said.

Rafiq seemed asleep but his eyes flickered when he heard them come in. It took him a while to get his bearings right and they looked at him eagerly. He smiled weakly.

"Ammi, how did I land up here?"

He sat up. Ruksana hugged him and sat beside him. Abdul and Nagma stood watching them with a mixture of contentment and apprehension. The needle of the saline drip came unstuck and Rafiq winced.

"It is all right, Beta," Abdul said. Rafiq looked at his father uncomprehendingly.

"How long have I been here?" he asked, looking around the room.

"Calm down. You have been here since this morning. You took sleeping pills and we rushed you here," Ruksana said.

Rafiq's mouth dropped. His eyes moved from his Ammi to his Abba, then to Nagma Khala and then to the ceiling.

"It is all right, Beta," Abdul said again.

"Will you stop saying that?" Rafiq blurted out. "You know it isn't."

Abdul flinched, as if he had been slapped across the face. Rafiq immediately regretted his outburst. He reached out a hand to him. A doctor came in. He told them Rafiq would be transferred to a psychiatric ward, and that since he was on bail the police would be involved with the discharge.

"He should be home in about ten days or so," he said.

"He was tortured in prison," Abdul said. The doctor noted something on a pad and nodded.

"You should inform your lawyer," he said. He pointed out that with the suicide attempt it was possible Rafiq's court case could take a different course. Then he proceeded with his morning rounds.

Nagma was ready to leave. "I will come tomorrow," she said and kissed Rafiq's forehead. "Everything will be fine. Allah will look after us."

Ruksana accompanied her to the door and gave her five twenty-dollar bills. "Take a taxi back. I wish I could pay you for both ways, but you know I can't. Here is some for returning." Nagma protested but Ruksana held her hand in a tight grip and looked at her pleadingly.

"Khuda Hafeez," Ruksana said.

"Allah Hafeez," Nagma replied and walked down the aisle, her gait unsteady.

Ruksana waited till Nagma turned a corner and then returned to the room.

Father and son shared an uneasy silence. Abdul was standing beside Rafiq, who was staring at the ceiling. Ruksana was worried that Abdul would make some careless remark about the morning or start a discussion. She knew Rafiq wouldn't want to talk about what happened.

"You should rest now. We will be outside," she told him.

"No, Ammi, both of you be with me. I don't want to be alone," Rafiq said softly and then glanced at his dad and added, "Abba, I'm sorry I got angry."

"Beta, it is all right. Oh, I am sorry, I forgot you don't want me to say 'It is all right,'" Abdul said and smiled sheepishly. He bent and awkwardly hugged his son. Rafiq smiled weakly, feeling secure in his father's arms. Suddenly he was a kid all over again, not the fiercely independent young man.

In the evening, Ziram came with Jameel. Both offered to spend the night at the hospital but Rafiq wouldn't let them.

"I'm OK. I wish I could go home now," he said.

The hospital staff told them that it wasn't necessary for any of them to stay overnight; Ruksana insisted on staying. Ziram and Jameel left, promising to come early next morning before going to work. Abdul left with them.

"You keep the cellphone, you may need it if there is an emergency," he said to Ruksana while leaving.

Abdul had never been alone at home, and loneliness added to his melancholy. He went to the washroom to have a quick shower and hoped to sleep early, but wandered about the house restlessly. He finally settled down to watch television. Close to midnight, he called Ruksana. She was awake and reading from the Quran.

"Go to sleep, Saabji."

"I can't," he said, and then began to sob into the phone. "I have failed everyone."

Ruksana didn't respond, because she knew that nothing she said would make him feel better.

"Why, Ruksana? Why us? We must have done something terrible for such things to happen to us repeatedly," he said, his voice shaking.

"Saabji, pray at dawn, you will feel better, go to sleep now," she told him.

Abdul was reluctant to pray but she insisted. "Saabji, there is nothing more to life."

Ruksana was sorry for her husband. Even though he tried to be tough on himself and stubborn and uncompromising with his family, he was emotionally fragile, unable to handle even simple tasks on his own. He was completely dependent upon her. This was the reason for his lack of success. For her husband, principles were all that mattered. She now admired his idealism. His lack of success had never mattered to her. She also realized, belatedly, that she had always unfairly compared her husband to Dhinmant.

Like most immigrants who end up with the proverbial short end of the stick, Ruksana had longed to return to her native home. She had wished to abandon their half-lives in Canada and return to India, to do something more meaningful than merely survive. She knew in her heart that Abdul might want that too. She wanted to go to Sarhupur to see what had happened to her hometown; and to Gorakhpur with Abdul to see the family with whom he had lost touch. But she also knew that they were never going back. Now they had the responsibility of looking after their son.

Abdul didn't go to the bedroom; instead he slept on the couch in the living room. Ruksana called him before dawn and asked him to offer the morning namaaz. It was many years since he had offered prayers but he hadn't forgotten; this surprised him, yet he didn't find it strange. Prayers brought momentary relief, however, the peace that he expected remained elusive.

Kartar and Harminder came with breakfast for him; as they were about to leave, the phone rang. Kartar asked in his heavily accented English: "Hello, yes please?"

"I want to speak with Abdul Latif," the person said.

"Who is speaking?" Kartar asked. The person did not answer. Covering the mouthpiece with his palm, Kartar handed the phone to Abdul, who took it and gruffly said, "Hello?"

"As salaam aleikum," the voice sounded urgent and respectful.

"Waleikum salaam," Abdul replied.

"We heard about Rafiq's suicide attempt and have called to offer our support. We are sorry for what happened to your son."

"Who is this?" Abdul asked sharply.

"A well-wisher of your family."

Abdul gripped the phone harder. It was one of Ghani Ahmed's men.

"I blame Ghani Ahmed for what has happened to Rafiq. Tell him that," he said forcefully, momentarily forgetting Ravindar's instructions that he was to remain calm and get more information. He struggled to control himself. "I can't hear you; I want to meet you," he said.

There was no response and moments later the line went dead. He called Ravindar and told him about the call. He learned that the police had been monitoring the phone and was relieved.

"They'll call again. I am sure about it. You just engage them for longer the next time they call," Ravindar instructed.

"I will try," Abdul replied. He glanced at Kartar and Harminder.

"We will drop you to the hospital," Kartar said. He was afraid that Abdul might have an accident if he drove himself, given his mental state. Abdul nodded absently.

Twenty-two

Rafiq was hospitalized for a week. His parents had come every day to be with him, often sat patiently by his bedside and in silence. Ziram and Jameel also visited every day. Nagma Khala came twice. The neighbours wished to come every day but Abba told Kartar Singh that was not necessary.

A day before Rafiq's discharge, Ziram told him of the phone call from Ghani Ahmed's man. He had called at home. Rafiq recalled that his cellphone was at home, either switched off or dead.

"Abba called Ravindar right away," Ziram said.

Rafiq nodded anxiously.

Ghani Ahmed was his past that he wanted to discard. But would it let go of him? The police case was founded on it. All he knew was that he was in a mess. What had the other members of the group said about him? They did not know him, but they could have lied to save their skins.

"I must call him one last time just to tell him that he shouldn't call again," Rafiq said.

"I don't think that's necessary. The court has clearly stated that you're not to do that," Jameel said firmly, and Ziram nodded in agreement.

Rafiq didn't want a long discussion about Ghani Ahmed. "You must come to take me home," he said to Ziram, to change the subject.

"I'll be at work."

"I can come," Jameel said.

"No, I'll take a day off," Ziram put in quickly, knowing that Rafiq wouldn't be completely comfortable with his brother-in-law.

"We'll both come," Jameel said. He didn't want Ziram taking all the burden by herself. He worried about her condition.

—⁂—

After they left, Rafiq read from the Quran. He felt a sense of calm, an inner peace enveloping him. His Ammi and Nagma Khala had often talked about the power of the Quran to bring peace to a disturbed mind. He agreed that the book had that power to bring tranquility, to lead one to the right path . . . but why then hadn't it kept him on the correct path? But perhaps it had, for in the end he had rejected Ghani Ahmed's plans. He had learned a lesson. For all it gave, however, he couldn't understand why anyone would want to read the Quran continuously, as his mother and Nagma Khala did.

They read from it daily, and when they finished the book, they started from the beginning. After years of doing so, they knew most of it by heart and could recite verses from it without looking at it. He had often argued with them that they were already experts in the book and didn't have to read the book over and over.

"You should read interpretations and arguments to have a better understanding," he had urged them.

Of course, neither his Ammi nor Nagma Khala did that. In prison, after repeatedly reading his favourite passages from the holy book, he had come to the conclusion that he had been both hasty and unfair in judging these two mothers, because in them he had seen serenity, an inner calm, an easy acceptance of their adversities, a centrality and rootedness—something he hadn't experienced ever. Perhaps there was merit in just reading and rereading the holy book. It must have a power. Like his dad, he was a troubled soul, never at peace, never calm.

He asked his parents about this contradiction.

Abba's reaction was predictable—that it was better to be troubled than to be fatalistic, and his Ammi immediately retorted, "If you believe in something then that is all that really matters. There are many ways to reach Allah. Some do it through the namaaz, some by reading the Quran, some by reading scholarly works, and many by merely following the right path."

His parents began to argue.

"Saabji, you preach tolerance, but do you realize that you are actually quite intolerant?"

"Yes, I do sometimes. I have little patience with purposeless piety because it prevents action. To accept everything in a resigned manner is fatalistic."

"There is little you can do to change your circumstance once you have decided on a course of action," Ammi said. "Often you can't retrace your steps, so constant action is not necessarily good. Prayer and reflection help in developing a perspective."

"You alone can change your life, and you can do it by being active, by questioning, not by accepting," was his father's comment.

Ruksana waved a hand at him to stop talking and, not wanting to upset her, Abdul became quiet.

"In all these years I have never won an argument with your mother about religion," Abba said with a wan smile.

Rafiq also smiled. He was an uneasy amalgam of his parents and in the last few weeks he had begun to acknowledge this duality. He didn't have to be either like his Abba, the perennial contrarian, or like his Ammi, the acceptor. But he was also questioning his own assessments of his parents. Was his mother really the quintessential Indian woman who accepted her fate quietly, silently suffering through her life? She definitely wasn't. In fact, she had fought her way through all her challenges in life and found a way to move ahead and improve her life. And was his father really the radical contrarian that he thought him to be? He may have been that in the past, at least that is what the family talked about—his power as a trade union leader. But that wasn't his memory of Abba. He knew his dad as a man who had toiled to make ends meet. Abba was like most dads—hardworking, dedicated to his family, unable to relate to his grown-up children, feeling misunderstood all the time and desperately wanting to be accepted and loved.

—⁓—

That afternoon, when Abdul and Ruksana were sitting half asleep in the lounge of the hospital, Nagma Khala arrived. When she saw Rafiq, she sensed his unease and anxiety.

"I have spoken to Kulsum. She told me the board members are not sure if they can hire you while the case is going on. They have asked their lawyer," Nagma said.

"I can work from home," Rafiq told her.

"Yes, we discussed that and Kulsum confirmed that it is OK."

Ammi came to check on them and smiled at Nagma.

"I was telling him that the centre may still hire him," Nagma said.

Rafiq wasn't sure his mother approved of the idea and explained, "They are checking with their lawyers about whether they can." But he was surprised to hear his mother say, "I hope they hire you."

"I can freelance if they can't," Rafiq said.

"Yes," Ruksana replied, but looked uncertain.

"Sab theek ho jayega, it will all work out," Nagma assured her.

She too sounded more hopeful than certain. Ruksana left them and Nagma sat quietly by Rafiq, looking up at him and smiling uncertainly. Her affection and concern, though seldom articulated, were palpable.

"Rafiq, your Abba said to the doctor that day that the police harassed you in the prison," she said.

"Not the police, other inmates; but I think they were all in it together—the prisoners and the cops."

Nagma didn't probe further and Rafiq didn't say more. After she was gone, Rafiq thought about his harassment in the detention centre. He had not talked about it to anyone except Anita and his parents because it had been such a humiliating experience. It had traumatized him further because of his inability to respond to them. He had been terrified. That memory could never be erased from his mind.

But he wasn't going to let it affect his attitude or his plans for the future. He reasoned that what he had suffered was payment for his involvement with Ghani Ahmed. His situation was ironic, but he knew it was one of the many things that had to be left behind as he tried to find a way forward, a way out.

Next morning, everyone turned up at the hospital—his parents, Ziram and Jameel, the neighbours, and Nagma Khala—and though he feigned annoyance, Rafiq was actually happy to see them all there for him. He was like a celebrity.

"Anita will be coming home this evening to discuss options. She seems confident of a positive result," Abba said.

That was good news. He was desperate to restart his life. He asked Ziram and Jameel to come home in the evening. He didn't want to be alone with his parents. His sister nodded. After completing the formalities at the hospital, Abdul and Ruksana brought Rafiq home.

Later, Anita arrived with a large bouquet of flowers for Rafiq. Ziram and Jameel were already there, and Ruksana made chai for everyone. Jameel greeted Anita affectionately and thanked her for helping the family. They had chai, and it was time to talk.

Anita smiled warmly at Rafiq before she began. "Hope you're feeling better," she said. He smiled weakly in return and nodded.

"So what do you suggest?" Abdul put in, impatiently. "Tell us what to expect now."

"We have a few options, but none of them are definite successes, and most will depend upon the cooperation of the investigation agencies," Anita said.

"I'll accept whatever you suggest," Rafiq said quickly. "I just want to be out of all this."

"It may not be that easy. You're going to be involved with this for a long time."

"So what are the options," Ruksana asked.

"We can argue that Rafiq needs psychiatric help and he was not responsible for his actions," Anita said, and looked at everyone in the room to gauge their reactions.

None were forthcoming.

"You can turn into an approver and help nail down the role of the real culprits in the conspiracy. We can offer that you will cooperate with the investigation agencies . . . and perhaps have you work in their covert operations."

Rafiq looked distinctly uneasy at these suggestions.

"We can go for a plea bargain, where you will agree to some of the charges against you for a lesser sentence," Anita said.

Rafiq nodded, but didn't know what to say. He looked at Abba and then at Ammi, but they were as clueless as him.

"He will do whatever you say. We don't know what would be the best for him," Abdul said.

"It's really up to Rafiq. Except for the first option, about Rafiq needing psychiatric treatment, every other option will require him to cooperate with the investigation authorities," Anita said.

"I don't really have any information that would be of any value to the investigators," Rafiq said. "They may not be interested in having me as an approver."

"The problem with all of these options is that it implies that you were involved with Ghani Ahmed," Ruksana said. "You have to say you are sorry and you have to assist them in their inquiries."

"They may require more from you . . . " Abba said.

"What more?" Rafiq asked. No one said anything, and he went on, "If any of the options can work in my favour, I think we should go ahead. But what does it involve? Will I go to prison still?"

"Yes, a very likely option right now. But that could change," Anita said. "We can bring accusations of torture, if necessary, and you will offer to cooperate . . . become an informer . . . "

"You mean spy on his community," Abdul said, grimly.

"If there is no choice. But he can always come out of that later . . . renege . . . First we have to make a deal."

Jameel and Anita chatted amiably about some mutual work they had done in the past. And then the visitors left, Jameel and Ziram for their apartment, and Anita for her office.

Rafiq went down to get his cellphone—it was dead. He plugged it in to recharge it and saw that there were several missed calls from an unlisted number. Ghani Ahmed's friends had obviously tried to call him first. A constriction built up in his chest, his breathing hardened and fear paralysed him, just as it had when he was at Thorncliffe centre talking to Kulsum. He called Ziram from Abba's phone and told her about Ghani Ahmed's calls on his cell phone.

"Please get me a new cell phone with a new number when you come this evening," he said.

"You're not supposed to have one. Are you OK?"

"Yes."

"Talk to the police. Let them know you got these calls."

"I will."

He wanted to flush his phone chip down the toilet but just then Nagma Khala called.

"I spoke to Kulsum. Her centre will hire you but you will have to work from home. They will pay twelve dollars an hour."

"That's great, Khala. Thank you."

When they hung up, Rafiq sat by himself pondering over his situation. He was lucky, he had support. He wanted desperately to rebuild his life. It wasn't going to be easy—it would need a lot of hard work. There were all the bad memories, of his abuse and his own stupidity, of the ordeals he had put his family through. But he had his beliefs, his faith. It had come to his aid, he was convinced of that. With their aid, he would steer a calmer, more sober path.

Acknowledgements

Nurjehan Aziz; Fraser Sutherland; Mahrukh Pasha Bhatt; Helen Walsh & Diaspora Dialogues; Farzana Doctor; Ali Adil Khan; Jasmine D'Costa; Sunil Rao; Joyce Wayne; Sanjay Talreja; Paul Dhaliwal; Pankaj Mehra; Dawn Promislow; Yoko Morgenstern; Sonal Shukla; and many other friends, relatives and well-wishers.

Thanks to Charles Pachter for permission to use *Decoy, self-portrait, 1966*, for the cover.

A special thank you to MG Vassanji for his guidance and friendship.